The Shadow Lantern

The Shadow Lantern

Teresa Flavin

A TEMPLAR BOOK
First published in the UK in 2013 by Templar Publishing
an imprint of The Templar Company Limited,
Deepdene Lodge, Deepdene Avenue, Dorking, Surrey,
RH5 4AT, UK
www.templarco.co.uk

ISBN 978-1-84877-941-9

Printed and bound by CPI Group (UK) Ltd, Croydon, CR0 4YY

For Alicia

Chapter 1

The Wee Cuppa Café was packed with chattering teenagers who had just escaped from nearby Braeside High School. Every seat was taken and the tables were covered with cups, crumbs and scrunched-up napkins. So many backpacks and wet jackets were piled on the floor that Ellie the waitress had to kick them aside with her foot as she bustled over to Sunni Forrest and Blaise Doran's table.

"What is it with you two?" she asked good-naturedly, as she put down another hot chocolate for Sunni and a second latte for Blaise. "Got no homes to go to?"

"It's Friday, Ellie!" Sunni said, inhaling the delicious fumes rising from her cup. "Besides, who wants to walk home through that?" She nodded at the wind and rain lashing at the café's picture windows.

"It's just a bit of weather." Ellie shrugged. "Or are you scared the ghosties will get you?"

"I think all the ghosties are in here." Blaise waved his hand at the Halloween decorations hanging on every wall and door. Ellie laughed and hurried away.

"And all the ghouls, too," said Sunni under her breath, looking sideways at a table of boys teasing a girl across the room. "Wonder how long it'll take Shug and his mates to start on us."

"Who cares? I sure don't." Blaise doodled in his new pocket-sized sketchbook. "Just ignore them."

Sunni sighed and watched him draw. He was so laid back she wondered whether he'd even notice if she wasn't there, and whether he'd care. She'd lied to her stepmum – again – about where she was going after school so she could be with Blaise, and sometimes he didn't seem to appreciate it at all.

"What are you doing tonight?" she asked, spooning whipped cream into her mouth.

"Aw, probably not much. Maybe watch a movie with my dad or something. What about you?"

"I'm going to Mandy's birthday party," she said.

"Oh, yeah?"

"Yeah. It's a sleepover."

"Bunch of girls then."

"So?"

"So… nothing." Blaise finally looked up at her. "I guess you're not grounded any more if you can go to a party."

"They're letting me go because she's my oldest friend." Sunni winced inside. She hated being dishonest but she didn't want to hurt his feelings.

"Then tell Mandy happy birthday from me."

"Okay." She sipped her hot chocolate to calm herself down. She got butterflies every time she saw Blaise now. It wasn't just because she was lying to him. That was awful enough. What hurt more was that he was always polite and friendly, but nothing more. Eight weeks ago in London they had almost kissed, but there was no sign of that happening again, thanks to Sunni's stepmum and dad.

We just want you to have a bit of a break from Blaise. That's how Dad had put it to her, but it wasn't what she had overheard her stepmum Rhona say to him. *That boy's father let them roam around alone in London and look what happened. Blaise took Sunni to the Starling House museum because a stranger told him it was cool – and they were kidnapped! He's a nice enough kid but he's not a good influence on her.*

Sunni hadn't been able to tell Blaise that her parents blamed him for getting them in trouble during their visit to London, so she had said she was grounded. After a while he stopped asking her when she'd be free to hang out again. That's when she started to lie to Rhona and her dad.

"What are you doing tomorrow night?" Sunni asked. "For Halloween."

"Not sure. Probably nothing. Maybe Dad and I will—"

"Watch a movie?" Sunni finished for him. "Two nights in a row?"

"Are you saying I'm boring?" Blaise grinned as he downed the dregs of his latte.

"No, it's just that Halloween is on a Saturday night this year! You should do something fun."

"I don't have a costume," he answered. "And it wouldn't be any fun without you there."

Sunni flushed. "I hate this. I wish I could do what I want, when I want." *And with whoever I want.*

Blaise just gave her a sombre smile. Then his gaze shifted to something behind her shoulder. He stared for so long that Sunni turned round to look.

"What is it?" she asked, noticing nothing but crowded tables and the windswept street outside the café windows.

"I'm not sure," Blaise said. "I thought I saw something – someone – hanging around outside, staring at us. But he's gone now, if it was a 'he'."

"There are lots of people out there," Sunni said. "Was it someone we know?"

"I couldn't see his face. He had a hood on."

"You don't think that we're being followed again, do you?"

"Who knows? That creep Soranzo had his spy follow us all the way from Braeside to London and we didn't notice." Blaise frowned. "Boy, was I stupid. I let Soranzo lure us into the year 1752 so he could kidnap us and try to make us tell him Fausto Corvo's secrets."

"But that's all over now. Soranzo can't mess with us again. He's stuck back in his own century," she said. "When we left Starling House, that painted door was closed and there was no way he could open it again."

"I know. But the guy in the hoodie could be one of his pals." He lowered his voice to a whisper. "Another slimeball who wants to find Corvo's lost magical paintings."

Sunni whispered back, "I wish we could just tell the world that we saw Corvo alive inside his painting at Blackhope Tower... and that those three paintings were with him. And that no one else can ever steal them because the only way in is shut forever!"

"Well, we can't tell anyone," said Blaise. "We promised Corvo."

Sunni remembered the sorcerer's last words to them. *You have witnessed the magic of the heavens, a miracle few have ever seen. That I have allowed you to see it means that we have a bind of trust. You are privy to my work and must help protect it.* She, Blaise and Dean were the only people, other than those still inside *The Mariner's Return to Arcadia*, who knew that Corvo had harnessed the power of the planets and stars to bring his drawings and paintings to life. And they knew that he had hidden all his secrets under the surfaces of the three most magical paintings he had ever created, making them precious to Soranzo. This greedy man would do anything to possess paintings he could slip in and out of whenever he wished – and where he could learn the secret of immortality.

"And we haven't told anyone," Sunni said, remembering how Soranzo had nearly killed them for defying him. "But he might not be the only one who thinks he can force us to say where the three paintings are."

"That's why we still have to be on guard."

"I really hope you're just imagining things," she said. "About the hoodie guy outside."

Blaise tapped his pencil against his sketchbook. "Me too. But it's not the first time I've seen someone hanging around."

A shiver ran down her neck. "What are you talking about?"

"It's happened a few times recently. He always vanishes before I get a look at his face," Blaise said.

"Don't go all spooky on me just as it's getting dark outside," Sunni said.

"I'm not trying to freak you out! I'm just telling you so you know what's going on."

"Great. I'll keep my eyes open for dodgy hoodies." Sunni

sighed, glancing at the wall clock. "I'd better go home or Rhona will be on my case. Are you coming?"

"My dad's supposed to pick me up here in a while." He glanced at the café windows again. "But I can walk you home."

"It's okay. I'll be fine on my own." The last thing she needed was for Rhona to see her with Blaise.

"Be careful."

Sunni pulled on her jacket. "Blaise, I only live two minutes away. I think I can manage."

"Okay, then don't be careful!" he said. "Sheesh."

Sunni bit her lip. "Bye. Guess I'll see you on Monday."

"Yeah. Have fun tonight. And happy Halloween."

"Thanks. Happy Halloween, Blaise."

As Sunni reluctantly left the Wee Cuppa she turned round to wave but he was bent over his sketchbook, lost in his own thoughts.

Blaise angrily rubbed out the sketch he was working on. *I can't do anything right today*, he thought.

He looked up at the café windows, but Sunni was long gone. She'd be home with her sniffy stepmum, Rhona, just where that lady wanted her – safely out of Blaise's company. He was pretty sure that Rhona blamed him for their London escapade by the cold way she'd acted towards him and his father when they arrived home with Sunni and her dad. No matter how many times she insisted she was still grounded, he knew Sunni was trying to spare him the truth.

He thrummed his pencil hard against the sketchpad. Everything was screwed up now. They had to sneak around like being together was wrong. And the worst thing was, he'd completely lost his nerve about kissing her. He knew he still liked her as much as ever, but did she like him in *that* way? He couldn't tell.

"Where's your girlfriend?" A sneering boy scraped Sunni's chair along the floor. "Gone off to fairyland again?"

Three boys surrounded the table.

"Naw, she's flown away on her broomstick," answered another.

The first boy squinted over Blaise's shoulder. "Draw us a pink unicorn like you saw inside that painting."

Blaise looked up briefly. "Give it a rest, Shug."

The boys guffawed.

"Go on," Shug said. "Draw it."

The other boys began a low chant of "Draw it, draw it".

Blaise flipped his sketchbook shut and sat up straight. "Get lost."

But the chanting went on and heads started to turn in their direction.

"I said to get lost." Blaise stood up to his full height.

The boys feigned being scared and continued to taunt him like grinning monkeys, glancing at the counter to make sure Ellie didn't notice.

Stand your ground. Blaise gritted his teeth. *Don't give them anything to use against you.*

Shug knocked Sunni's empty cup over and hooted.

All of a sudden, a host of masked figures appeared at the boys' backs and a female voice cackled, "These numpties will boil up well in my cauldron. Plenty of blubber for us all!"

The creatures laughed and the boys stopped chanting.

"What's wrong, wee man? You've got a face like a burst tomato," said the witch from behind her mask. Shug snorted and elbowed her in the ribs. She rubbed her side and hissed something at him in a low voice.

The tallest figure, disguised in a furry purple animal head, clamped a hairy paw onto Shug's neck and said in a deep voice, "Beat it, all of you, or Ellie will ban you for life. And she's far scarier than us."

The boys swore but they stalked to the exit, kicking bags and knocking into people. Shug made an insulting gesture and disappeared into the dusk.

Blaise looked round at his rescuers. "Um… thanks."

The witch pulled her mask off and he recognised Iona, one of Mr Bell's art students from a couple of years above him. "No bother."

The others shed their masks, grinning. They were all older kids whose artwork he'd seen displayed in the school corridors and school exhibitions, but they'd never talked to him before. The tall one in the fur mask turned out to be the impossibly talented James, who everyone said was destined for great things.

"Eejits. They wouldn't dare try it on if they weren't in their little posse for courage," James said, scratching his chin with a furry claw. "I should have lined this mask with something. It itches like mad."

"You made that?" Blaise asked.

"Yeah. I'm into making masks at the moment," said James. "Handy for this weekend."

"You going, Blaise?" asked Iona, shaking out her shiny copper-coloured hair and tossing a leaflet onto the table. "It's the Enigma Festival at Blackhope Tower."

For a moment he was taken aback that she even knew his name but then realised it must be for the same reason everyone else did – his disappearance last winter at Blackhope Tower. But she had spoken to him in a friendly way, unlike some people at Braeside High School who didn't believe they'd been pulled inside Fausto Corvo's painting that day.

"I heard about it," he said, eyeing the leaflet. "But I'm not sure."

"Because of what happened to you there?" asked Iona.

"No." Blaise felt himself going red. "I just don't like crowds."

"I get you," said Iona, and the others nodded. "But this festival is going to be cool. Mr Bell's in charge of all the decorations and they look amazing."

Blaise knew some Braeside High teachers had volunteered to help with the festival, including his art teacher, Lorimer Bell. "Yeah, he mentioned it during a lesson."

"We made a lot of the decorations after school." Iona nodded at the leaflet. "And James did the artwork on this, too."

"It's excellent," said Blaise, smiling approvingly at the flying witch on the cover. He glanced at the information inside and was about to hand it back when he read something that made him catch his breath.

"If the festival gets a lot of visitors they're going to do one every year," said James. "Mr Bell says they've got some big names to do talks and stuff. There's even this one guy who's going to take photos of Blackhope Tower's ghosts."

"Umm," Blaise murmured, only half listening as he reread the announcement that had just taken him by surprise. "Sounds good."

"Oh, it will be," said one of the girls. "There's a fancy dress party tomorrow night."

"Uh-huh." He had to speak to Mr Bell as soon as possible. Apart from Sunni, his art teacher was the only person who would understand.

"It's getting late," said James, stuffing his mask and paws into a backpack. "We'd better head over there now."

Blaise looked up and blinked. "Isn't Blackhope Tower closing soon?"

"Yes," said Iona, "but they'll let us in to help finish decorating. Mr B's up there already."

Blaise handed her the leaflet but she shook her head.

"Keep it," she said and joined James, who was already moving towards the exit.

"Would it be okay for me to come along and have a look?" Blaise asked hastily.

James threw a glance over his shoulder. "You mean now?"

"Yes," he replied. "But if it's not cool, no problem."

Iona shrugged at James and the others. "Why not?"

Blaise phoned his father as he trailed them out of the café. "Hey, Dad," he said in a low voice. "You don't need to pick me up at the Wee Cuppa. I'm doing something with some people from school. No, I'll get home by myself. Fish and chips would be awesome. I'll phone you when I'm on my way."

The night was sweeping in on a vicious west wind. A dead leaf hit Blaise in the back of the neck and he whirled round, ready to fight. He walked backwards and watched the empty road behind them for signs of someone following. The hedges and drives were black and silent but he imagined the silhouette of a jacket hood could move into view at any moment, skimming past the light of a window like a shark's fin.

Chapter 2

"Hey!" Dean's hoarse voice called. "Where've you been?"

Sunni backed up two steps and stuck her head into the front room. "None of your business."

Her stepbrother was slouched in her dad's leather chair, eyes glued to a screen, poking and prodding game controls. He swore and continued jabbing.

Sunni shook her head and carried on walking towards the stairs. With every inch Dean had grown this year, his attitude had increased with it. He was now much taller than she was and never stopped reminding her of it.

"You weren't with Blaise, were you?" Dean taunted.

"Like I said," she called back wearily, "my business, not yours."

"That's a yes, then."

Just ignore him, Sunni said to herself. But that's what she'd been doing for weeks. She turned on her heel and stalked into the front room.

"Get a life, Dean!" she said. "You're like some old grannie sitting here all the time, watching who comes and goes. It's just sad!"

"Me, sad?" Dean wore a smug little grin. "Go look in a mirror, Sunni."

"That's out of order—"

"Oh yeah?" he cut in. "At least I'm not permanently miserable. And like I really care where you've been when you act all secretive."

"You seem to! You jump on me every time I walk through the door."

"Because you're going to get caught soon," Dean smirked. "And I want to be there when Mum finds out. Which she will, 'cause you haven't got the guts to stand up for yourself."

"What a cheek!" Sunni stared at him. "I had enough guts to come and rescue you inside the painting last winter."

"Yeah." Dean shrugged. "That was then…"

"I'm not listening to this." She swept out of the room before he started needling her again.

"Is that you, Sunni?" Rhona asked from her bedroom.

"Yes."

"What time are you going to Mandy's?"

"Soon."

"How are you getting there?"

"Walking."

"I'm not so sure about that…"

"I am."

She locked her bedroom door and threw her bag onto her bed. *You haven't got the guts to stand up for yourself.* Dean's words sat in her head, refusing to budge. The longer they sat there, the angrier Sunni got, because maybe her annoying stepbrother had a point.

Her Halloween costume was hanging on the back of the door. It wasn't her most original idea to be a ghostly maiden, but it was easy. Still fuming about Dean, she took her outfit and make-up into the bathroom, emerging twenty minutes later in a white vintage nightgown, shawl and flat shoes. Her face, lips and arms were chalky pale and her long white wig made her look like she'd stepped from a snowdrift. Her eyes were darkly circled with grey eye shadow.

She put her pyjamas, a change of clothes and Mandy's birthday present into an overnight bag and tiptoed carefully downstairs. She could hear Dean in the front room and went out through the back door so she wouldn't have to see him again.

"I'm off," she shouted back into the house. Rhona's voice buzzed a question from upstairs, but Sunni just answered, "I've got my phone. See you tomorrow."

The wind blew the thin gown up over her knees and she held the wig down as she made her way along the dim street. The rain had stopped but she had to step around slimy piles of leaves and twigs. Something behind her made a cracking sound and she nearly tripped over an uneven paving stone as she turned round.

What if Blaise is right and we are being followed? She squinted into the gloom but saw nothing. It couldn't be Soranzo. He was back in the 1500s where he belonged, but what if someone else was after them?

A car's headlamps cut through the darkness and it slowed to a halt by Sunni. A vampire girl in the back seat rolled down the window.

"Sunni?" she shouted and opened the car door. "It *is* you. Get in, or you'll ruin your costume."

"Vicky! Nice timing." Sunni heaved a sigh of relief and climbed inside.

"You should have phoned me. We could have picked you up."

"I thought I'd walk it," Sunni said. "Dean's been driving me mad and I needed to calm down."

"What a surprise," said Vicky, rolling her eyes. "You look so cool, Sunni. For a minute Mum and I thought we were seeing a real, live ghost."

"There's no such thing as a live ghost."

"Whatever," said Vicky. "Your jacket and bag gave you away."

"Real ghosts don't need to carry their pyjamas about." Sunni grinned. "Nice fangs, by the way."

The two girls jumped out of the car in front of a stone house with leering jack o' lanterns glowing in each window and a skeletal scarecrow flapping at the gate.

The main door swung open by itself. Mandy's front hall was completely dark and silent.

"Oh, no, here we go," Vicky whispered. "Her dad's up to his old tricks."

"Yeah, you can see it coming a mile away." Sunni took a step inside, her hands up in front of her face to ward off whatever was coming. "Hello? Mandy?"

Vicky was moving ahead, close to Sunni's side, when someone right next to them screamed and something whizzed through the air. A tangle of sticky, stringy stuff hit Vicky in the face and she shrieked, batting it away.

"Ewww!" she shouted, her voice nearly drowned out by the piercing screams nearby. "Get it off me!"

Sunni yanked Vicky sideways and stumbled forwards. She put her hand out to feel for a wall or furniture and grasped something like a railing. But it felt plasticky and moved slightly.

"Oh no, Vic," she murmured, as the thing came away from whatever had been holding it in mid-air.

"What?" Vicky managed to ask in between nervous giggles.

Before Sunni could answer, a torch flicked on, revealing Mandy's dad in a Frankenstein costume. He held the light under his chin, making his face shadowy and horrible, and then flashed it at them.

"Arm," he grunted, waving one empty sleeve. "Give me my arm."

Sunni gaped at the bloody arm in her hand and dropped it to the floor with a screech.

There was a fragrance of wood smoke in the air and the dense trees swayed in the dark as Blaise followed James, Iona and the others up Blackhope Tower's long drive. He chatted and laughed with them, but dark memories of this castle were flooding over him.

The place had had an eerie reputation for centuries because of its connection with the artist Fausto Corvo, who was also suspected of sorcery. In 1582, Blackhope Tower's owner, Sir Innes Blackhope, paid Corvo to make him a special painting, *The Mariner's Return to Arcadia*, which hung in the Mariner's Chamber. The artist also designed a notorious tiled floor-labyrinth for the chamber before he vanished mysteriously. Ever since it had been constructed, skeletons had appeared suddenly on the labyrinth with no explanation.

Blaise had known the rumours that Corvo had made magical paintings and had escaped Venice to protect his artwork from being stolen by rich and greedy Soranzo. But he would never have imagined that *The Mariner's Return* was also a magical painting and that the labyrinth would transport him to the heart of it, into the wondrous but deadly worlds of Arcadia, on that unforgettable afternoon.

Iona broke into his thoughts. "Have you been at Blackhope Tower a lot since… you know?"

"Off and on," he replied. "But everything's different in the Mariner's Chamber now. You can't get up close to see the painting any more."

"I know. It's total rubbish!" James said. "Lucky you got inside it while you could."

Yeah, lucky me, Blaise thought. *I get to worry whether criminals will be after me for the rest of my life.*

"I'd love to know what it was like to be inside *The Mariner's Return.*" One of the girls got into step with him. "I know a lot of people at school think you made it all up but I believe you."

"Uh, maybe later?" He didn't want to talk about it, and his attention was attracted to a row of marquees on the lawn in front of Blackhope Tower. They glowed from inside like paper lanterns and he could see a few people lugging equipment back and forth from cars and vans. The tall stone castle loomed behind, dotted with lights in its small, deep-set windows.

The girl shrugged. "Oh, okay."

She left him and caught up with James, who led them into Blackhope Tower's entrance hall and told the lady behind the reception desk where they were going.

"I reckon Mr Bell will be up in the Great Hall," said Iona as she skipped ahead of James to the spiral staircase. They wound their way up the narrow stone steps to the first floor, following the hum of voices.

Blaise stopped short at the Great Hall's entrance. "Wow."

"It's good, isn't it?" Iona grinned.

The enormous room had been transformed into an atmospheric cavern. A canopy of giant black spider webs hung overhead, a vast net below the grand vaulted ceiling and brass chandeliers. Stags' antlers and ancient shields were still mounted high on the walls but the rest of the paintings and decorations had been taken away to make room for large black silhouettes of flying witches with tattered robes trailing behind them and grinning skeletons dancing hand in hand. A row of tiny jack o' lanterns, carved out of turnips, lined the windowsill of the large window in one wall, waiting to be lit. The huge walk-in fireplace contained the largest pumpkin Blaise had ever seen. Mrs Gordon, a maths teacher at Braeside High, was hunched on a stool sawing a face into it.

She let out a puff of air. "Mr Bell! The wretched thing has defeated me. Can you give me a hand please? This pumpkin refuses to become a jack o' lantern."

"I'll do it, Mrs Gordon," said James, striding over.

She shook her head. "I'm sure you'd do a lovely job but let's not risk a visit to A&E, hmm?"

Lorimer Bell called out, "Just give me a moment. I'm caught up with the web." He was balanced on a ladder, tying a long-legged felt spider into the web with a piece of elastic.

"Blaise," he said with a smile as he caught sight of his pupil. "What are you doing here?"

"I came with the others to have a look." Blaise nodded at James, who was now walking around with several other spiders bouncing up and down from his fingers. "That web is amazing."

Lorimer pulled on the spider to make it dance and climbed down the ladder. "Made by Iona and her crew. Don't ask me how they did it because I think it involved witchcraft.

And crocheting many, many balls of black wool with gigantic hooks."

"Can I help?" Blaise asked.

"Hmm, let's see," his art teacher said, scanning the volunteers arranging round tables and folding chairs. His eyes rested on a woman in a flowing dress tacking a skeleton silhouette to the wall. Strands of her long dark hair were dyed violet and indigo blue. "I'm not sure…"

"Anything."

"That's very kind, Blaise, but I think we're sorted with helpers in here."

"Okay." Blaise touched the festival leaflet in his pocket and his heart began to thump a bit faster. "But do you have a minute to talk? I need to show you…"

"Oh, Mr Bell," said Mrs Gordon sharply. "The pumpkin?"

"One moment, Mrs Gordon," Lorimer replied. "What is it you need to show me, Blaise?"

"Can we go outside for a second?" he asked, dropping his voice.

"Of course." Lorimer led him outside the Hall's door and asked, "What's the matter?"

"This." He pulled the leaflet out and pointed at the block of words that had caught his attention.

Lorimer glanced at it and nodded. "The Oculus. I saw that, too."

"Do you know anything about this, Mr Bell?" asked Blaise.

"Nothing more than it says here," said Lorimer. "A fellow called Munro is going to exhibit a magic lantern designed by Fausto Corvo called the Oculus."

"Yeah, Fausto Corvo!" Blaise said breathlessly. "Since when did he design magic lanterns?"

"It was news to me too, but not that surprising when you think about it. Corvo created paintings and labyrinths but he also designed sculptures and even the rapier he carried."

"I guess it is the kind of thing that would interest him." Blaise stuffed the leaflet back into his pocket. "But this came out of nowhere. Some guy's just turning up with this Oculus and showing it off in the Mariner's Chamber…"

"Where everything happened to you last winter." The art teacher nodded sympathetically. "Is that what's really bothering you about this?"

"Yeah, maybe," said Blaise. "It feels wrong. Why can't people gawk someplace else? Why can't they just leave the Mariner's Chamber alone?"

"I've sometimes felt the same way after what happened to Angus." Blaise saw a shadow cross Lorimer's face at the mention of his crooked cousin, Angus Bellini, who had pursued them into *The Mariner's Return to Arcadia*.

"Sorry, Mr Bell. I didn't mean to remind you..."

"Don't be sorry," said Lorimer. "It wasn't your fault. Angus brought everything onto himself. But you and Sunni and Dean returned safely, thank heaven, and the labyrinth faded to nothing. It can't take anyone else away now."

"It must be weird for you to be here doing this festival."

"Because of Angus? Sometimes. I'd give anything to have him back, even after what he did, because he's still my flesh and blood. But I'm learning to accept what I can't change, Blaise," Lorimer said. "It might sound a bit strange, but when I'm here, at least I can go to the Mariner's Chamber and say hello to him. I know he's somewhere deep inside that painting."

"I talk to my grandmother at her grave," murmured Blaise, and as soon as he said the word 'grave' he wished he hadn't. Angus wasn't officially dead, though he might as well be. "Oh man, I'm sorry."

Lorimer laughed under his breath. "Don't worry. I know what you mean, though Angus would hate being compared to anyone's grannie." He rubbed his hands together. "Now then. Aren't you a little curious about this magic lantern Corvo designed?"

"Sure."

"So am I," said Lorimer. "I'll be having a close look at it myself when I can get away from festival duties. Speaking of which, I'd better get back to that pumpkin." He turned to leave. "You coming, Blaise?"

"No, I think I'll head home."

"You're not going to hang out with Iona and James and the others?"

"They're pretty busy. Maybe I'll see them tomorrow." Would he? Had they even noticed his absence from the Great Hall? He had no idea. "Good luck finishing up tonight, Mr Bell."

"Thanks, I think we're nearly there." Lorimer smiled. "And you're okay, right?"

"Yes," Blaise answered. "Guess I just needed to talk."

"Good. Safe home then."

Blaise's mind was racing. He took a few hesitant steps down the spiral staircase then turned round and sprinted up to the next floor.

The corridor was empty and silent. He crept towards the Mariner's Chamber, hoping it might be open for last-minute festival preparations. An elaborate sign outside proclaimed that Munro would be displaying the Oculus at regular times throughout Saturday and Sunday, plus a Halloween show on Saturday night, but for now the door was firmly shut.

As he walked away, Blaise tried to let go of his uneasy feelings. For all his teacher's soothing words, he still worried about the arrival of Corvo's invention. Where had it come from? And why had Fausto Corvo made a magic lantern at all?

Blaise swung down the narrow staircase and hunched into his collar as he crossed the entrance hall. When he hit the outdoors he broke into a jog and set off along the drive past the marquees. The wind hit him square in the face and he had an unnerving moment of déjà vu. Eight months before, he'd left Blackhope Tower alone one snowy late afternoon and walked this route with his head full of another problem. He had tossed and turned all that night trying to decide whether to go into *The Mariner's Return to Arcadia* to find Sunni and Dean. And he'd despised himself for taking so long.

A new ball of emotions was now spinning inside Blaise. Blackhope Tower was drawing him back, if it had ever let him go. Part of him wanted to run the other way but another part wanted to know about this Oculus.

He leaned into the wind and pushed on. By the time he reached the bus stop on the main road, he knew what to do.

Chapter 3

The six girls at Mandy's sleepover party burst into the dining room, which was lit with candles and lanterns. A feast was laid out on a black tablecloth decorated with silver moons. The vampire, ghost, elf, witch, zombie prom queen and alien filled their plates and hurried back to the living room to snag the best seats.

Sunni had just settled down to a plate of tacos and salad when someone tapped her shoulder. She nearly dropped her dinner when she saw it was the plastic arm with a bloody stump instead of an elbow.

Zombie prom queen Mandy laughed and waved the plastic arm as she plunked herself down on the sofa next to Sunni. "Recovered yet?"

"Just about. That thing nearly gave me a heart attack."

"We got you this year!" said Mandy triumphantly, smoothing down her ruffled dress with a gloved hand. "I thought you were going to faint." She patted Sunni's knee with the plastic arm. "Hey, if I put a pen in its hand, it can write. Maybe it can even do the Ouija board for us."

"Will you get that away from me? It smells as bad as it looks."

"Hmm." Mandy raised it to her nose. "Can't smell anything. Guess I'm used to it."

"Used to it? Like it's part of the family or something?" Sunni bit into her taco with a crunch.

"Yeah. My dad puts it in funny places as a joke. This morning it was holding the shower curtain back."

"Ugh," said Sunni. "Are we really doing the Ouija board? They're kind of creepy."

"Not to me," said Mandy.

"Well, you hear stories about what happens when people mess about with them—"

"I don't mess about. I do the Ouija board properly."

"Okay, okay," said Sunni. "I believe you."

When they had sung happy birthday, eaten the carrot cake with poisonous-looking orange icing and cooed over Mandy's gifts, the girls cleared away the remains of the feast and brushed down the black and silver tablecloth.

Mandy unfolded a piece of velvet on the table and lifted out a thin board with letters, numbers and the words 'Yes', 'No' and 'Goodbye' printed on it. She took a flat, tear-shaped object called the 'indicator' out of a little muslin bag and laid it on the board. It had a circle cut out of the middle, like a peephole.

"This Ouija board was my great-gran's," she announced. "She was psychic."

The girls let out 'oohs' and leaned in close to examine it.

"Did spirits talk to her when she used this?" asked Kirstie, her painted green alien face intent.

"Yes." Mandy was as solemn as a high priestess. "And they've talked to me and my cousin, too."

"No way!" said Vicky, her mouth hanging open slightly. "You've never said anything about it."

"Only my closest friends know."

The girls all smiled at each other.

"I don't want it going around school," Mandy warned. "You know what some people are like. That idiot Shug and his pals, for instance." She glanced at Sunni. "I heard he was torturing Blaise at the Wee Cuppa this afternoon. But that guy James who's always getting awards and Iona with the rust-coloured hair came along and rescued him."

"Really?" Sunni could hardly believe this. James was in his final year and didn't usually bother with any of the lesser life forms in the years below.

"Blaise went to Blackhope Tower with them after that," Caitlin piped up.

Sunni flushed when she realised they were all staring at her. "So? I don't know anything about it. Can we just get on with the Ouija board, please?"

"Sunni's right," said Mandy. "Now, be quiet and listen to everything I tell you."

Sunni only half-listened. Blaise had told her he was going home after she left, not to Blackhope Tower. What was that all about?

She snapped back to the present when Mandy asked loudly, "Do you want to ask the spirits a question or not, Sunni?"

"Er, okay."

"Then you'll go third after Vicky and Kirstie. Better think of one now."

Mandy placed the indicator on the board and swept her arms in circles over the table.

"I'm about to invite the spirits in and I don't know

what will happen because it's so close to Halloween. By tomorrow night, there'll hardly be any boundary between our world and theirs," she said ominously. "If they have any messages for us, they'll move this indicator onto each letter to spell out words. But it's easier for them if they can just answer 'yes' or 'no' to your question."

The girls shifted in their seats and suppressed nervous giggles until Mandy glared at them and crossed her arms over her chest. When they finally quietened down, it was so silent Sunni could hear the grandfather clock ticking in the front hall.

Mandy moved her arms in circles again, asking, "Is there a spirit here with us?"

She touched the indicator lightly with her fingertips and closed her eyes. Slowly the object moved up to the word 'yes'. There was a sharp intake of breath around the table.

"What is your name, spirit?"

The indicator swept from letter to letter spelling out N-E-L-L.

Mandy smiled broadly when someone whispered the name out loud. "Nell, you're back! She comes every time I do the Ouija board. She always tells me stuff."

The girls were frozen in their seats, hardly breathing.

"It's my birthday today, Nell," said Mandy. "Guess how old I am."

The indicator danced away from her fingers and spelled out a word by itself. FIFTEEN.

The girls let out low cries of astonishment. Mandy opened her eyes and glanced gleefully around the table.

"I told you they talk to me," she said. "Are there any other spirits with you today, Nell?"

ONE.

"Ooh," she said. "Who is it?"

The indicator didn't move.

"No problem, Nell, we like talking to you. Ask your question then, Vicky," said Mandy in a hushed voice.

Vicky was transfixed. Kirstie nudged her and she jumped, saying each word clearly as if the spirit were hard of hearing. "Will I pass my exams?"

The indicator moved off YES for a second and then jumped straight back onto it.

Vicky hugged herself and whispered, "Oh, thank you, Nell!"

Kirstie leaned over and said slyly, "Here's my question, Nell. Does Caitlin fancy Robbie?"

Caitlin looked embarrassed and watched the board intently. The indicator slid across the board to NO.

"See, I told you I didn't, Kirstie!" she said in a low voice. "Thanks, Nell."

Mandy frowned and said to Sunni, "Your turn."

"I'm not sure what to ask you, Nell," Sunni said.

The indicator flicked violently and spelled out NOT NELL.

"Oh, Nell's gone away," said Mandy, looking a bit startled. "Welcome, spirit. What is your name?"

The indicator stayed still.

Mandy nodded at Sunni to ask her question. Sunni licked her lips and tried again. "Will you tell us your name, spirit?"

The indicator slid down to the letter I. The girls hardly breathed as it zigzagged to S, H, B, E and finally L.

"Ishbel," Sunni said in a choked voice. "*Lady* Ishbel?"

The indicator zoomed onto YES.

"Do I know you?"

YES.

Everyone stared at Sunni.

She swallowed hard. Of all the people from beyond the grave, she had attracted the attention of the one whose death she had accidentally caused. Flashes of that awful moment were burned into her memory. Sunni, Blaise and Dean had been trying to escape from Arcadia, the treacherous world below Corvo's painting, *The Mariner's Return to Arcadia*. As Sunni walked around the labyrinth that would transport her out, Lady Ishbel Blackhope had jumped onto her back, trying to force her to give back a map she mistakenly thought Sunni had. When Sunni ended up half-conscious on the floor of the Mariner's Chamber, the other girl's skeleton lay at her side. Lady Ishbel had lived for over four hundred years inside the painting she had inherited from her great-uncle Sir Innes Blackhope and could not survive for even a moment in the twenty-first century.

"What do you want?" Sunni whispered, unable to take her eyes off the Ouija board.

The indicator stayed where it was. No reply.

A question floated up from the back of Sunni's mind and she blurted, "Is someone following me?"

YES.

She could barely get the word out. "Who?"

At that precise moment Sunni's phone vibrated loudly against the wooden side table it sat on. The indicator leapt off the Ouija board, which started spinning madly. Mandy's presents, so neatly stacked on a sideboard, smashed to the floor.

"Sunni!" Mandy shrieked. "Take that phone out of here and turn it off now!"

The indicator was coming straight at Sunni like a missile in mid-air as she scooped up her phone. She darted from the dining room with it pressed to her ear, shouting, "Yeah?"

"Sunni?" Blaise sounded far away on the other end. "I need to talk to you.'

"Can't talk now," she panted and slammed the door behind her. "Everything's gone mad here!"

Chapter 4

By the next day the gales had moved on and the Enigma Festival was in full swing under bright autumn skies. Blaise strolled round the wooden walkways that had been laid down to keep people off the muddy lawn, waiting for Sunni to show up and tell him what on earth had happened the night before.

He wondered if James or Iona and the others were about but there was no sign of them. The food marquee was heaving with people clutching Halloween-themed biscuits and hot drinks so he walked out again. The book marquee had a long queue of fans waiting for a famous horror writer to sign their books and he gave that a miss. When the woman he'd seen last night with the violet and blue streaked hair floated past him into a tent marked 'Mysteries and Curiosities', he decided to follow.

The large tent was cramped with elaborately decorated stalls and displays of curiosities. Blaise avoided the man waving booklets about how the treasures of the Knights Templar were secretly buried in Scotland and another proclaiming that Blackhope Tower was built on an energy line that made people disappear into an unknown dimension.

In the far corner Blaise could see a familiar silhouette

of a witch dangling from the ceiling. To get to it he had to push past displays of strange talismans and a fortune-teller's cubicle draped with long scarves. He got caught in a crowd next to a musty walk-in cupboard of vintage clothes, but squeezed through and came to a stall that said, 'Aurora Midnight, Maker of Hand-cut Silhouettes'. Its walls were hung with scores of small black oval frames containing miniature profiles of people and animals. Next to her stall were two clothes rails crammed with large silhouettes hanging from coat hangers by pegs.

Blue-and-violet-haired Aurora sat at a table covered in scraps of paper, snipping with long-handled scissors at the silhouette of a cat. Now that he was there, Blaise wasn't sure what to say. But she sensed his presence and looked up.

"Hey," she said with a smile.

"Hi." He ventured up to the railings and leafed through the silhouettes. "These big ones are cool. I mean, they all are, but especially these."

"Thanks." She put her work down and asked, "How would you like your silhouette done?"

"Me? Oh, I don't have enough money with me to…"

Aurora laughed. "No, for free. It attracts customers if I make a silhouette of someone posing. They love watching." She gestured towards an empty chair in front of a big sheet of cardboard. "If you sit there I can see your profile better."

"Sure," said Blaise shyly. "Is it okay if I text someone?"

"Of course," she said. "Just sit still while you're doing it."

While he fiddled with his phone, Aurora selected a piece of paper that was white on one side and black on the other.

She cut into the white side, her eyes flicking back and forth between Blaise and her work. The paper moved this way and that as she formed his chin and nose, the flick of his hair over his forehead and the shape of his skull. Within two minutes she had finished a perfect silhouette the size of his hand.

"Wow, that was fast! And you didn't even draw it out first," Blaise said as he examined it.

"That's part of the magic." Aurora's eyes sparkled. "Can I do another one? Some people are wandering this way."

"Yup." He looked at the wall of miniatures as he posed. "Is that Mr Bell up there? Did you make one of him?"

"You recognise him? Yes, he was one of my victims, I mean, models," she said with a laugh. "We've known each other a very long time. Since high school, actually."

"Really? He's my art teacher."

"You're lucky. He decided to stay in Braeside and make a difference while I went off to wander the world." She held up another finished silhouette. "I haven't been here in years. But I came back after I heard about Angus and stayed on."

Blaise stiffened. "You know Angus?"

"We were all in school together." Aurora laid down her scissors. "He was a good pal."

Yuck, Blaise said to himself. *That's hard to believe.*

"Wait," she said. "How do you know about Angus?"

His face must have had the answer written all over it even though he said nothing. Aurora squinted at him and said, "You're Blaise, the boy who went into the painting. I've seen your picture."

Blaise fidgeted in his seat. "I don't really like talking

about it if you don't mind. Sorry, but I'd better get going."

"Oh my goodness. Of course, it must have been so traumatic for you. I completely understand." She swept out of her seat and blocked his exit. "You can't imagine how often I've wished I could speak to one of you. I'm so desperate to know what happened to Angus."

"Didn't you ask Mr Bell about him?"

"He doesn't know any more than the newspapers," she replied, an unspoken plea in her eyes.

Actually, we told him everything but he's cool enough not to spread it around. Blaise peered past her, hoping some lurking customers might divert Aurora, and was relieved to see Sunni storming towards the stall.

He waved and said, "My friend's coming. I have to go."

"Oh, not yet," she said. "I'll do you another silhouette – a bigger one."

Sunni appeared, waving her phone. "Couldn't we have met in the food marquee, Blaise? Some weirdo's been trying to sell me love potions for the last fifteen minutes."

"Hi." Blaise didn't want to say her name in case Aurora cornered them both. He got up from the chair and tried to edge around her. "Um, excuse me, ma'am."

"I'll make a silhouette of you, if you like," Aurora began, turning to Sunni.

But at that moment a black cat jumped up onto the table and sat staring in Sunni's direction with its tail curled round its feet. The markings on its face were disconcerting. It was as if a white X was painted across its eyes and nose.

"Hel-lo," Sunni said, putting her hand out to pet it. "You've got a funny face. But cute."

The cat recoiled from her touch and continued to stare at a point just above her shoulder.

"What's it looking at?" asked Blaise.

"I don't know," said Sunni. "Let's go."

"Oh no, wait. Don't move," said Aurora, searching the people milling nearby and finally spotting someone. She called out, "You'd better come. Lexie's seen something."

"*What* is going on?" Sunni whispered fiercely, watching the motionless cat. "Can we get out of here now?"

"Yeah, come on." Blaise took a step but a soft male voice said, "Be very still, miss. Just for a moment, please."

A dapper showman in a derby hat, paisley vest, tight trousers and narrow, pointed boots hurried towards them. He was enthusiastically strapping on a pair of antique goggles with purplish lenses. "Thank you, Aurora. How long has Lexie been there, would you say?"

"Less than a minute," said Aurora.

"Might be something," said the man hopefully. "Or might not. Please don't move a muscle, miss. Be very still…"

Sunni stayed put but looked none too pleased about it.

He sidled up to the table and murmured, "What do you see, old girl? Eh, my lovely? Somebody there?"

Blaise saw Sunni's face go from annoyance to shock in three seconds. "Uh, mister, can you please—"

The man put up one hand in apology while the other slid a sleek little camera from the watch pocket of his vest. "I'm very sorry about this, but would you mind if I take a few pictures? Just a couple. If you stay very still…"

He hesitated long enough for her to shrug and began snapping pictures of Sunni and the empty space beside her.

"That's enough," said Sunni, jumping away.

The atmosphere broke and Lexie the cat turned her head sideways to look up at the man.

"Well, that's that." He sighed and unfastened his goggles. "I'm sorry, miss, but there wasn't time to explain what I'm doing. I have to shoot pictures while I can because my subjects don't tend to hang about for long." He produced a card from another pocket in his vest and handed it to her.

"Munro, Spirit Photographer," she read aloud.

"I've heard about you," murmured Blaise. This oddball was the guy who was showing off Fausto Corvo's Oculus.

"Only nice things, I hope." Smiling, Munro doffed his hat and produced a cat treat from another pocket. He placed it in front of Lexie and caressed her head. "My good lassie."

"I still don't understand," said Sunni.

"Just one moment..." Munro studied the photos he'd taken and his eyes lit up.

"Did you catch a spirit?" Aurora asked breathlessly.

"I do believe I have." He turned to Sunni. "Did you feel a presence behind you just now?"

"No."

Blaise could see Sunni tense and he moved closer to her.

"Would it surprise you to know that a presence was on your back a few seconds ago?"

A presence? A chill ran down Blaise's neck. *But there was nothing on Sunni's back...*

Sunni's eyes were wide with alarm. "Yes," she said in a small voice.

But Blaise could tell that wasn't true.

"Ah. I know this sounds very odd," Munro said gently. "But do you have any idea who it could be?"

"I'm sorry, but you're freaking me out." Sunni grabbed Blaise's arm and dragged him back into the warren of stalls. He felt her hand quaking as he glanced back and saw Munro waving after them.

"Sorry! Just give me a chance to explain," the spirit photographer called.

"Come back sometime, Blaise!" added Aurora Midnight.

Sunni shot him a sidelong glance. "That woman knows your name?"

"Just by chance. She recognised me for the usual reason. Are you okay?" he asked.

"I need air."

They pushed their way out of the tent and Sunni urged him towards the woods behind Blackhope Tower. They squelched over the wet lawn, taking in deep breaths of crisp air, and followed a path that meandered through dense trees covered in orange and gold autumn leaves.

"I have got to tell you something!" Sunni said as she jumped over a boggy piece of ground.

"Yeah, me too! But you go first, you've kept me waiting since last night." Blaise kicked a rotten branch out of his way. "Why couldn't you tell me on the phone?"

"Things were crazy at Mandy's, and then I didn't get home till lunchtime today. And I need to tell you face to face so no one hears." She shivered. "Oh, Blaise, I am so freaked out."

"Will you please tell me what's happening? You're driving me nuts." The spiked iron fence around a small overgrown graveyard came into view and Blaise stopped. "Wait. Why are we coming here?"

"It's quiet." She pushed through the gate. Even in the dappled sunlight, the mausoleum and crumbling tombstones were dank and melancholy. "And I need to look for something."

"Sunni." Blaise caught hold of her arm and said sternly, "Tell me what's going on!"

She let out a long breath. "Something weird happened last night. We fooled around with a Ouija board at Mandy's. She invited spirits in and all that. At first she was guiding the pointer thingy that spells out the spirit's answers, but it took off by itself and spelled out the name Nell. It really was a spirit! Mandy had talked to it before."

"Come on. You believe that?"

Sunni moved close to the mausoleum with BLACKHOPE engraved above the rusted door. She tried to peer into its dark interior through a tiny barred window but sank down and perched on the step.

"Blaise, the pointer was moving by itself, answering our questions," she said. "It even spelled out the number fifteen when Mandy asked it how old she was. I'm telling you, Mandy *is* psychic but she's been keeping it secret. I had no idea till last night."

"Yeah, well," he scoffed, picking at a piece of ivy growing over the mausoleum door. "Then what?"

Sunni's head dropped. "Another spirit came in and took over when it was my turn to ask a question. The pointer went so jumpy it nearly scratched the board when it spelled the name out: Ishbel. *Lady Ishbel* from Arcadia."

"What!"

She nodded mournfully. "Yeah. I even asked if it was her and it answered yes."

"This has to be a trick. Mandy must have been controlling that Ouija board secretly," said Blaise. "Or someone was helping her."

"No. Whatever was controlling that thing wasn't human," Sunni said, her eyes wide. "So then I asked if I was being followed and the pointer said yes."

"Why did you ask that?" Blaise's stomach clenched. "Didn't the girls want to know why?"

"Yes, but I gave them some story that I'd seen a shadow in the road. I just wanted to know if you're imagining things about the guy in the hoodie," she said. "Guess maybe you aren't."

"Okay, so now the whole world knows." He swatted the ivy, annoyed. "Then what happened?"

"Just as I asked it who was following me, you phoned and everything went mad. The Ouija board spun round, Mandy's presents went flying and the pointer came after me. Somehow Mandy calmed Ishbel down and made her go back to wherever she came from. Her dad's banned her using the Ouija board and now she's got the hump with me."

"Oh boy," Blaise groaned. "My phone call kicked that off?"

"I guess. Ishbel wasn't one of your greatest fans either, since you took the map she wanted when we were in Arcadia."

"Her spirit knew it was me on the phone?" He snorted. "And it wasn't *her* map. She thought she automatically owned everything in Arcadia, but *I* found it."

"It doesn't matter," said Sunni. She looked back over one shoulder and shuddered. "Lady Ishbel's got her hooks into me now."

"You think that because of what happened in the tent? Munro just saw something on your back. He didn't say it was a girl."

"What else could it be but Lady Ishbel?"

"You didn't wait around to see the photo," Blaise said. "We only have his word for it."

"I don't know." Sunni chewed on her thumbnail. "I can't get Ishbel out of my head now. The last time I saw her, she had turned from a living girl to a skeleton in seconds."

"I know," Blaise soothed. "But you'll drive yourself crazy if you keep thinking of that."

Her voice shook. "She's buried somewhere in this graveyard, right?"

"The news said her skeleton had been buried here in the family cemetery."

"Probably in this mausoleum, right?"

"I guess," said Blaise. "I don't see any new gravestones."

"So aren't spirits supposed to be at peace if they've had a proper burial?" she asked glumly.

"You should have asked that question at your séance." Blaise shrugged. "Maybe there's some kind of spirit rule book."

"Thanks a lot. This is serious, Blaise," Sunni muttered. "I asked her spirit what it wanted but it wouldn't answer."

He threw up his hands. "Sunni, you've got to get Ishbel out of your head."

"Her spirit might be right here listening," she said.

"Fine. She can listen all she wants. We've got other stuff to do." He checked his watch.

Sunni rubbed her face and slowly straightened up. "Like what?"

"Have you had enough air?"

"Yeah."

"Good. Let's get out of here," said Blaise, striding towards the gate. "This place gives me the creeps even in daylight."

"I'm not going back to that tent..." Sunni jumped to her feet and hurried after him.

"We aren't. Come on, we've got somewhere else to go!"

Chapter 5

Sunni could happily have gone home, leaving Lady Ishbel and Blackhope Tower behind. Instead she was marching up its spiral staircase and down a familiar corridor.

"What did you tell your dad and stepmum you were doing today?" Blaise asked.

"The truth." She jutted her chin out. "That I was going to the Enigma Festival."

"And they let you?"

"They didn't like it at first but I told them this festival was educational."

He laughed. "Educational!"

"Yeah, why not?" Sunni said. "Mr Bell's here and other teachers are too."

"Fair enough." Blaise grinned.

She made a face. "But you never said we had to go to the Mariner's Chamber."

"You hung up so fast last night I couldn't tell you anything."

"And you still haven't!" she said. "What did you want to tell me?"

Blaise didn't need to answer. When Sunni saw the sign announcing Munro's Oculus show times she almost turned on her heel to leave.

"Not him again," she said, coming to a halt.

"Yes, him, but not for the reason you think," Blaise said.

The door to the Mariner's Chamber was cracked open but there was no light within. Sunni saw the end of a row of folding chairs and heard a few voices murmuring.

"It's about to start." Blaise nearly pushed her inside and she scrambled onto a vacant chair. She could just make out people's forms in two rows of seats around her. Otherwise the chamber was black except for the hurricane lamp in Munro's hand, a mysterious glow at the centre of the room and a large flickering image of a familiar raven silhouette projected on the wall.

Blaise slid into the seat next to her.

"Why is Fausto Corvo's raven symbol up there?" Sunni hissed into his ear. "What's going on?"

"I don't know. That's why we're here," he said.

Munro's newly jacketed and top-hatted figure darted into the corridor and flipped the sign round to say 'Performance in Progress' before hurrying back inside and closing the door. The lamplight cut a path through the dark until it reached the glow in the middle of the room. Atmospheric music rose from somewhere in the background.

"Welcome to the Enigma Festival," Munro intoned, holding the hurricane lamp up near his face. "I am Munro, photographer of spirits and collector of antique curiosities from around the world. And this" – he set the lamp onto a tabletop next to a glowing metallic object – "is the Oculus, a magic lantern invented by the extraordinary artist Fausto Corvo. For centuries there were vague rumours that he had made what he called his 'shadow lantern' but it was as mysterious as Corvo himself. We only knew of the Oculus because he drew a sketch of it. Few people, if any, ever saw the completed lantern."

Sunni leaned in close to Blaise. "Did you ever hear about this before?"

"Don't think so," he whispered. "I might have seen the sketch but I can't remember."

Munro loomed in the low light. "The Oculus disappeared into the mists of time, forgotten, until I chanced to discover it in a curiosity shop in Istanbul. The shopkeeper hadn't a clue what it was, and nor had I until I had bought it and examined every inch. It was then that I realised I possessed one of the oldest magic lanterns in existence. I had a duty to share the Oculus with the world, and what better place to start than in the infamous Mariner's Chamber, home of Corvo's masterpiece, *The Mariner's Return to Arcadia*?"

The audience breathed out an 'ah' as Munro carried the hurricane lamp up to the painting, catching colourful fragments of people, houses and sailing ships in its moving light.

Sunni caught her breath. The painting's vivid cityscape looked so innocent but she knew first-hand the wonders and dangers that existed below the surface in the under-layers of Arcadia.

"This was the painting Corvo made before he vanished in autumn 1582," Munro explained. "It is said he was on the run from a rich, greedy merchant called Soranzo, who wanted three magical paintings that Corvo refused to sell. It was said they contained the wisdom of the universe –

and even the secret of immortality! But where the paintings are now, or if they even exist, is a mystery."

We know where, Sunni thought. *They're safe inside The Mariner's Return where no one can ever get to them.*

"And here on the floor" – Munro stamped his foot in the dark – "there was once a black-tiled labyrinth designed by Fausto Corvo. Skeletons appeared on it from out of nowhere. Last winter, the skeleton of Lady Ishbel Blackhope appeared and the labyrinth vanished. She was the great-niece of Sir Innes Blackhope, who built this castle, and she'd been missing since 1600. Another deep mystery."

"You didn't mention that three local kids were found with her skeleton," said a man in the audience. "The ones who went missing here and claimed they were inside the painting."

"Kids with good imaginations," grumbled another. "I'll give them that."

A couple of people chuckled and Sunni shrank into her seat.

Munro ignored the interruption. "And now, the new mystery of Corvo's Oculus. What exactly is this 'lantern of shadows'? On the face of it, it's just a simple projector. It's called Oculus, which means 'eye' in Latin." He held his hurricane lamp above the Oculus so the audience could see it. "One lights a wick in an oil container inside, sticks a painted glass slide in this slot and the image appears on a wall in a dark room. The smoke goes up out of the little chimney so it doesn't smother the flame. Simple."

He set his hurricane lamp back on the table, just out of

sight, and Sunni heard clicking and sliding sounds over the rising background music.

"And what of the glass slides?" Munro asked ominously.

As Corvo's symbol vanished, drums rumbled and a hideous painted demon popped up on the wall, shimmering and leering.

A few audience members gasped.

"Medieval devils," Munro called out as the demon vanished. The slides clicked and clacked in and out of the Oculus as he presented a macabre show. "Girls in glass coffins. Skeletal horses. Bats. Skulls with wings. Reapers. People of the past loved to be frightened just as much as we do today."

A crude image of a grinning skeleton appeared, a scythe held high above its skull. A gust of air whistled from a gap somewhere and sent the oil flame jumping. The skeleton seemed to dance in the flickering light, its black eye sockets staring straight at Sunni.

"Is this Fausto Corvo's work?" asked Munro, his voice rising again above the drums. "No! These crude painted slides were made later by craftsmen whose names are long forgotten. They were projected by travelling showmen in their magic lanterns."

The reaper vanished and the drums died down.

"But *this*, ladies and gentlemen," said Munro, "is one of three glass slides painted by Fausto Corvo. The detail and colour are so fine it could not have been painted by anyone else." Unlike the others, this one made no sound when he inserted it. It slid into place and a square of colours and shapes appeared on the wall showing part of a richly furnished but empty room.

Sunni nudged Blaise's arm excitedly.

"I know, I know," he whispered. "Corvo definitely painted that. You can tell."

Munro showed two more exquisitely painted images. "There doesn't seem to be anything mysterious about the three glass slides Corvo painted to go with his Oculus," he said. "As you can see, nothing's frightening about them – no monsters, no ghouls. They've no figures in them and tell no obvious stories. I cannot help but wonder if there is something more to them than meets the eye."

"So do I," murmured Sunni.

"Maybe the spirit of Corvo is looking down on us at this moment, laughing at our ignorance," said Munro in a wheedling tone. "Let's see if we can unravel the mystery of the Oculus. I invite you to share your theories with me if you'd like to stay and have a closer look at the lantern of shadows. Thank you."

Munro got a smattering of applause as he turned the overhead lights on and extinguished the Oculus and the hurricane lamp. As her eyes adjusted, Sunni looked round and a flicker of repulsion ran through her. The windowless plaster walls were a cold white under the ceiling lights and *The Mariner's Return to Arcadia* seemed to rule the chamber like a king on its throne. Since last winter a rope barrier kept people from getting too close to the painting that had swallowed up Sunni, Blaise, Dean and Angus and hidden them below its surface. And somewhere in the stone floor there might still be an echo of the labyrinth that had transported them there, but its black tiles had vanished.

"What do you think?" asked Blaise, stretching his legs below the seat in front of him. "Stay or go?"

"Stay," Sunni said, seeing the light of interest in his eyes. "He's got my attention."

"Yup, me too."

One or two people chatted to Munro and examined the Oculus but everyone else wandered away, leaving the door slightly open.

"Hello again," said Munro, recognising them with a rueful smile. "I'm glad you're here because I want to apologise properly." He appealed to Sunni. "I didn't mean to upset you earlier. I get muddled sometimes and don't explain things very well. When I catch sight of a spirit, I become completely caught up with it."

"I wish I could say I understand that, but I don't." Sunni noticed him looking over her shoulder, as if he were searching for another presence. She sat forwards, uncomfortable. "I take it the spirit's not hanging about right now or your cat would be staring at me."

Munro was sheepish. "No. And Lexie would notice if she were. So would I." The cat was curled up underneath a chair, sound asleep.

"Without your goggles?" asked Blaise.

"The amethyst-coloured lenses make the spirits stand out better but I don't have to wear them."

"Can I look at the photos you took?" Sunni asked.

"Ah, well. My camera's locked away at the moment but I can tell you she was a young lady with long red hair, wearing old-fashioned clothes from another time and a pendant around her neck."

Sunni's face tensed at his accurate description. I can't see the photos?"

"Of course you can. Tomorrow. I'll print them out and put them in my display in the Mysteries and Curiosities tent," Munro said. "But I have a feeling you don't need a photo to know who I just described. Am I right?"

She nodded.

"How long have you known she's with you?" he asked.

"Only since last night," Sunni answered slowly. "After my friend did the Ouija board."

"And invited in the spirits so close to Halloween." He shook his head. "Your red-haired companion heard the call."

"I wish she hadn't. How do I get rid of her?"

Munro inhaled deeply. "Not easy to answer that. She's chosen you for a reason."

"Whatever it is, she's picking on the wrong person," said Sunni, but at the back of her mind she suspected Lady Ishbel's spirit knew exactly what it was doing. Ishbel had openly disliked her in Arcadia, especially when she learned that Sunni had been in the company of Fausto Corvo's handsome apprentice, Marin.

"Did you communicate with her?" asked Munro.

"Well, I asked a few questions but we didn't get too far because we were interrupted." She glanced pointedly at Blaise. "She doesn't like the sound of phones vibrating."

"What do you think Sunni should do?" Blaise asked Munro.

"Go about your business as best you can," suggested the spirit photographer, "and try to put it out of your mind. The spirits will be lively until midnight, but then they'll start to fade away."

back where she belongs?” asked Sunni.

ll,” said Munro.

ded at the magic lantern. “Can we have a look

Oculus while we’re here?”

“Of course.” Munro swung himself out of his seat and ushered them to the table.

The shadow lantern’s box-like body was engraved with stars, angels and flying birds and had an arm with a glass lens set into its outer end like a telescope. Munro pointed out a hinged door on the back of the lantern and opened it, squinting as if he were looking into a doll’s house. A half-burned wick floated in the oil lamp fixed to the floor of the lantern and the ceiling was inky with soot, even though there was a little chimney sticking out of the top.

“Any theories about Corvo’s glass slides?” Munro asked.

"I'm not sure," said Blaise. "Maybe they were just scenes of places he'd been."

"Like holiday photos? They seem a bit dull for that. A bit of a room with no one in it?"

"They must have been interesting to Corvo or he wouldn't have made them," said Sunni.

"What else did you find out about the Oculus?" asked Blaise.

"I think it was made for Corvo in Amsterdam by a metal smith called Henryk de Vos. His initials, *HV*, are engraved in the bottom. It came in this trunk." Munro pulled a battered wooden chest out from under the table. A few words were painted in gold above a keyhole in the side. Some letters had worn off but Sunni could make out the word *Oculus*.

"There's a false bottom where I found this box holding Corvo's slides."

He showed them an empty silver container with words engraved inside its lid.

"Looks like Latin," said Sunni.

"It is," said Munro. "And it says something intriguing. The rough translation is 'Leave the light and travel the shadowlands'."

Sunni looked closely at the silver box. "This looks like it holds more than three slides. Are there some missing?"

"I don't know," answered Munro. "But you're right, they do rattle around a bit in their case."

"You didn't mention any of this in your talk," said Blaise.

"Ah no, I didn't," Munro agreed. "I've been talking with two Corvo experts in Venice and we've decided I should keep some information private until they've analysed the slides. The Oculus and I will be heading to Venice on Monday, when the festival is over." He lightly touched an engraved star on the lantern's body. "I haven't had the Oculus long and I wouldn't want someone nicking it."

"You're taking a risk bringing it here then, aren't you?" Sunni asked.

"I won't let anything happen." Munro glanced towards *The Mariner's Return to Arcadia* and went on. "When the managers of Blackhope Tower got wind of the Oculus, they were determined to have it as an attraction this weekend. How could I resist coming to this famous place for a couple of days?"

Blaise scratched his head. "If you're keeping the message on that silver box secret, why are you telling us?"

"You're not planning to run off with it, are you?" He grinned and took off his top hat. "No, seriously, I have a confession to make." The smile faded. "Aurora Midnight told me your name, Blaise. And who you are."

Sunni could see her friend was struggling to keep his temper.

"It's none of her business," Blaise muttered. "She shouldn't have said anything. I don't even know her."

"Then I have to apologise again." Munro laid his top hat on the table, revealing dark slicked-back hair. "I told you about the inscription because I thought you might be able to help decipher it. You probably know more about Fausto Corvo than all the experts in Venice!"

"Well, I've got no clue what that inscription means," said Blaise shortly.

Munro put his hands up. "Fair enough, Blaise. It was just a thought." His gaze shifted to the Mariner's Chamber door and at first Sunni thought he must have seen another spirit, until she clocked the annoyed look on his face.

At that moment, the wooden door slammed shut and Sunni could hear the sign outside clattering to the floor.

"What the—" Munro scrambled to the door and hauled it open. He darted outside and shouted, "Stop right there!"

Chapter 6

Sunni and Blaise reached Munro's side in time to see a dark hooded figure duck out of the long corridor and down into the stairwell. Blaise set off after him, leaping onto the first stone step just as he heard thumping footsteps below, then a clatter and an outcry.

A woman's voice wailed, "Watch where you're going!" and a man called, "Sir! Sir, do not run down the stairs!"

Blaise wound down to the landing below and came to a halt where an older lady was being helped to her feet by a guard. He bent down to assist them, but the guard gave him a suspicious look.

"I'm not having any stupid games in here, son," he said angrily, as he guided the lady to a chair. "No chasing your mates, no—"

"He's not my mate and it's no game, sir! That guy was messing around and I was trying to stop him."

"You leave that to us." The guard growled a description of the hoodie into his two-way radio.

What's the point? The creep's gone. He'll just pull his hood off and blend in with the crowd. Blaise jogged half-heartedly up the stairs and trudged back to the Mariner's Chamber.

Sunni and Munro were waiting outside.

"Any joy?" she asked.

"Nope. He was long gone."

"Thanks anyway, Blaise," Munro said. "Your friend told me you think you've seen him before."

Blaise kicked a stone floor tile with his toe. "I think so, but I might be wrong. It was dark before."

"I thought he might have been playing a prank," said Munro. "It's the second time I've caught him hanging about and he's run off."

"Did he say anything to you before?" asked Blaise.

"No, he was nosing about at the door. I don't like it," said Munro, adjusting his sign in the metal stand. "I'm going to have to keep this door locked whenever there's a break between shows, even if I'm inside. Better to be on the safe side."

"Yeah," Sunni and Blaise mumbled in unison.

"Well, you'll probably want to be on your way. Sorry again." Munro gave them a slight bow. "Stop by the marquee tomorrow if you want to see my spirit photos."

"Wait," Blaise said quickly. "I'd like to see Corvo's slides projected again, if you have time."

"I would too," Sunni added.

Munro took a pocket watch from his waistcoat. "I've got plenty of time before the next showing." He pulled the door firmly shut behind them and said, "If you don't mind being locked in for a few minutes."

"Fine by me," said Blaise.

"Me too," said Sunni. "And by the way, I'm Sunni. If you don't already know, I'm the girl who went into the painting with Blaise and my stepbrother Dean."

"No, I didn't know." Munro raised his eyebrows and smiled.

"Pleased to meet you, Sunni." He opened the Oculus's door, lit the wick and picked up a stack of small wooden squares. "These are Corvo's glass slides. They have the Roman numerals I, II and III painted on the frames."

He took the first one and slid it into the slot in the Oculus's neck. "Can one of you turn off the lights please?"

Sunni flicked the switch and the dark wall exploded into colour. Blaise carefully felt his way closer to the projection, fascinated with the scene before him. The slide showed part of a large medieval tapestry with a carved stool on the floor below it. A torch on the wall blazed in the dim space.

"I've been trying to identify where this room could be but it's impossible," said Munro. "I guess it's late sixteenth century because that's when Corvo lived. I found a stool like that in a book and it's Italian. The tapestry is older, I think."

Blaise edged up to the wall, close to the flickering projection. The jewel-like colours and delicate work stunned him. How had Corvo been able to paint the tapestry's complex hunting scene onto a small piece of glass?

"Look at the tapestry, Sunni," he said. "It's a little like that one we saw at the Victoria and Albert Museum." He stepped into the light to get closer. His shadow was hard and black behind him as he pointed at the tapestry. "See the hunting dogs?" he asked, smiling back in Sunni's direction.

The light dazzled him and tiny black shapes blinked in front of his eyes like dancing pinpricks. The black shapes multiplied even when he looked away and the blood began to rush to his head. Blaise hadn't felt this odd since he'd walked the labyrinth and been transported into *The Mariner's Return*. He thought he might pass out and yet he was completely solid on his feet, unable to move. He was somehow aware of energy curving and spinning around him, along with the strange sensation that layers of his body were peeling away and flying off into the darkness.

The feeling lasted only a few seconds. When Blaise opened his eyes, he could not talk. He knew what he wanted to say to Sunni and he lurched forwards to grab her hand. He started to speak, but she wasn't there.

He spun round, trying to make sense of where he was, and fell over something low and hard. Struggling to his feet, he gaped at the thing in his hands: a carved wooden stool. Slowly he looked up. Dancing torchlight lit the embroidered tapestry before him. He was inside Corvo's glass slide.

"No!" Sunni cried out. "No, not this! Please!"

This could not be happening. Blaise could not possibly have transformed into dancing particles of light before her eyes – but he had. And those particles had mingled with the light beaming from the Oculus, that fancy tin can on the table. Then she saw what looked like a swarm of fireflies hovering in the projection on the wall, starting to form the shape of a teenage boy. Blaise emerged fully remade, glowing at first around the edges, and stumbled round in the projection as if he had forgotten how to walk. He was working his mouth, saying something as he fell over the stool.

Munro's stunned voice came out of the dark nearby. "Oh no, no, no. This isn't possible. He was standing right there!"

"And now he's not," said Sunni with a catch in her throat. "That lantern has taken him apart and put him back together inside the slide!"

"I had no idea it could do this!"

"Fausto Corvo made these slides. That means *anything* can happen," she said tersely. "He was a magician who could bring his own paintings to life!"

"All right, what should I do?" Munro asked. "How do I get him out?"

"No clue." There was a chill at Sunni's back and the faintest whisper of a sound at her ear.

In the projection Blaise looked around him. His expression was alert but uncertain.

"I don't think he can see us," said Munro. "This is unbelievable." Sunni heard his fingers drumming on the table. "I'm going to turn the overhead light on."

"No! We won't be able to see him then." Sunni couldn't take her eyes off her friend.

"Okay, okay. Let's just stay calm and think of what to do next."

Blaise was staring at something they could not see, his mouth open in surprise. His lips moved but Sunni had no idea what he was saying.

"Something's in there with Blaise," said Munro. "I think there's more to this projection than we can see."

The whisper came past Sunni's ear again. *Ahhhhh.* She was aware of a touch to her jumper, as though a fly had landed on one stitch and sat there, waiting. She flicked at the spot but there was nothing there.

"This is beyond me," murmured Munro.

"Maybe Blaise will see a way to get back…" Sunni said. *But how long can we just sit here and watch?* The answer came into her head, hazily at first. *For as long as the oil lasts.* "The oil! How much is left?" She edged closer to the glowing Oculus. The magic lantern gave out more heat than she had expected.

"I'll check." Munro opened the door and squinted inside. "There's plenty."

"But what will happen to Blaise when it's gone? If the flame goes out?"

"I won't let it go out. Don't worry about that."

Blaise was inching towards the edge of the projection. With one more step he would leave it and vanish somewhere they could not see.

"What are you doing, Blaise?" she nearly screamed. "Stay where we can see you. Don't go anywhere else!" Again there was a slight depression in Sunni's jumper, as if a fingertip was pushing the fibres in. She scratched at her shoulder.

Munro's voice cut through the gloom. "Sunni, we can't wait. I'll have to go in after him and you'll have to keep watch here."

Ahhh. The whisper circled round her ear and she felt a finger of air on her back, then another, and another, until five encircled her left shoulder as if to comfort her. But there was nothing but malice in the feathery touches.

Sunni's blood turned to ice and she couldn't move. She was aware of a slight change in the light but could not lift her head.

"Sunni!" Munro said sharply.

She opened her mouth again and tried to make a sound.

A new feather of air touched her right shoulder. So light, and yet she thought it would go straight through to her flesh. She waited for the next touch and then the next, her mouth hanging slack.

Ahhh. The whisper circulated around the Mariner's Chamber like a whistle through bones.

Sunni could hardly breathe. Something was wrong with the Oculus's light. Everything was getting darker, like she was gliding into a tunnel. She inched her head sideways. From the corner of her eye, she saw the projection on the wall fading as the shadow lantern dimmed slightly. All she could think about was Blaise. Sunni could imagine him stepping out into cold blackness never to return.

"Sunni, what is going on?" Munro fumbled with something in the dark.

Suddenly Sunni spun round, nauseous at the thought of what clung to her back, and battled to dislodge the airy fingers from her shoulders.

"Get off me!" she shouted. "Leave me alone and go back where you belong!"

Ahhhh, came the spiteful whisper.

A small flame burst into life. Munro held his hurricane lamp high and peered worriedly at her.

"Be very still…" he began in a low voice, his eyes fixed on a spot just above her shoulder.

"I can't!" Sunni clawed at her shoulders. "It's her!"

Before she could get another word out, the fingers

released her and a keening gust of air spiralled round the room. It choked the hurricane lamp's flame and circled the Oculus, rattling its door.

"No, spirit!" Munro shouted. "I ask you, please do not interfere with the lantern! A boy's life is at stake."

Ahhhh. The phantom fingers worked the door open, reached inside the lantern and grasped the wick, smothering it until it sputtered into a smoking stump and the chamber went black. *Ahhhh. Haaaa. Haaaa.*

The wind subsided and the chamber went silent. Sunni lunged towards the table, colliding with Munro and falling back. "Get the Oculus back on. Please!"

"Matches, matches," he murmured.

Sunni heard the matches roll around in their box as Munro tried to get it open. She groaned with him as he dropped it and they scattered. Her heart racing, she shuffled towards the light switch, but tripped over chairs and hit a wall. She felt her way along the cool plaster surface with her fingertips, cursing every moment the Oculus was unlit.

Sunni's ears pricked up. A deep sigh and a scrabbling sound came from the other side of the chamber.

Something in the dark was sliding itself along the floor towards them.

Chapter 7

With a hard clicking sound, electric light flooded the Mariner's Chamber.

"Blaise!" Sunni exclaimed, her expression a mix of happiness and relief. She was huddled against the wall, one hand still on the light switch and facing the place where the scraping noise had come from.

Blaise was sprawled on the tiled floor, trying to turn over and get up, with Lexie the cat sniffing round him. He finally managed to get his mouth to say something. "Uh-huh."

"You got out of the slide!" Munro was on his hands and knees, surrounded by scattered matches. "That's a relief!"

"I think the projection spat me out," Blaise said.

Sunni and Munro were at his side in a flash, propping him up.

"Are you okay?" she asked.

"Yeah." Blaise smiled but he wasn't sure he was quite himself yet. "It was a close call though. I couldn't see any way to get out and I had no clue what to do. How did you get me back?"

"The flame went out and there you were," said Sunni.

"Mr Munro!" A gruff male voice called from the other side of the Mariner's Chamber door. "Is everything all right in there?"

"Jimmy…" Munro called, exasperation in his voice. "Everything's fine."

"Visitors reported hearing loud voices."

"That's right," said Munro. "All part of the Oculus events. I'm trying out something new."

"I see," said the security guard.

"As I told you earlier, Jimmy, some unusual things might happen while I'm here. Best not to worry if you hear a noise or see the odd thing on your security monitor this weekend."

"Fair enough. I'll leave you to it then." The guard's footsteps faded away down the corridor.

Munro turned back to Blaise, looking concerned. "Something in the slide spooked you," he said. "We could see your face but we couldn't see what it was."

"I was just gobsmacked to be in another of Corvo's magical worlds," he answered.

Sunni shook him gently by the elbow. "Are you really all right?"

Blaise blinked. "Yeah, I'm better now. Did you see what happened to me when I was transported?"

"How could we not?" she asked. "You started glowing and then you turned into a jumble of blinking lights! It was like your body was short-circuiting and sending off sparks. Then all your sparks just blended in with the light from the Oculus and you reformed inside the projection."

"Wow," Blaise said, examining his hands. "Maybe that's why my hands and feet are still tingling."

"You're not all right," said Sunni. "Maybe we should go."

"No!" He sat up straighter.

Munro grasped him by the shoulder. "Come on, let's get you into a chair."

Blaise managed to stand up and walk by himself. "I'm fine," he said. "Those floor tiles are freezing."

"What did you see in there, Blaise?" asked Munro, taking a seat beside him.

"I'm not a hundred per cent sure, but I know one thing. The projection is alive. The stool's real, the flame in the torch – all of it."

"Any idea *where* you were?" asked Munro, a rapt look on his face. "I'd love to know that."

Blaise exchanged a cautious look with Sunni. He knew she must be bursting with questions and he wished Munro wasn't there so he could tell her exactly what he'd seen.

"Just a room in a fancy house," he said. "I didn't see any more of the place than that."

"But you looked like you were about to go exploring," said Sunni. "You were almost at the edge of the projection and I thought you were going to vanish!"

"But I didn't. I'm right here."

"Thank goodness. So I own a painted glass slide that comes to life when it's projected," Munro said with a bemused smile. "I'm the one who's gobsmacked now."

"Maybe the other two slides are magical too," said Blaise.

"Maybe…" said Munro. "I'm certainly going to find out for myself."

"It's easy to get in on your own," said Blaise quickly, "but someone will have to help you get back, right? Like you guys helped me, blowing out the Oculus's flame."

"We didn't do that. It blew out by itself. Sort of," said

Sunni, glancing over her shoulder. "But I'll tell you about that later."

"I'll have to ask someone very trustworthy to stand guard," said Munro. "The Corvo experts in Venice will be keen, I'm sure. Unless they demand to go in themselves!"

"Don't you want to have a look now, while we're here?" asked Blaise.

"I could, couldn't I?" Munro murmured, gazing at the Oculus.

Blaise took a deep breath and avoided looking at Sunni. She probably wasn't going to like his next suggestion and her stepmother would hate it. "Or *I* could go back. I know what to expect from Corvo's worlds and you don't."

"What?" Munro put his hands on his hips. "Five minutes ago I thought you were gone for good. If I let you do that again, I'd be in such deep trouble..."

"It really wasn't a big deal for me. I got back and I'm fine," said Blaise in his deepest, firmest voice. "You told us about the inscription on the silver box because Sunni and I are 'experts' and you thought we could help, remember? Well, I do want to help – by finding out what's going on in that slide projection." Sunni was leaning forward with her head resting on her knuckles, strangely quiet. "I'll be able to tell you everything you need to know."

"No," said Munro. "I'm glad you stumbled onto this but I can't let you go back in."

"I could come to your next show and just walk into the light again." He knew he was pushing it but he had to get back inside the projection and see more. "Then it would be my fault, not yours."

"Blaise, what are you getting at?"

He shrugged. "I'm just saying, anything could happen."

"I've said no, but you'll go inside anyway?" Munro had one eyebrow raised high. "Then I'll have to bar you from my Oculus shows."

"That wouldn't look very good, would it, when I haven't done anything wrong?" Blaise asked. "Especially since everyone knows me. Sunni and I have special status at Blackhope Tower because we put this place on the map last winter. They've been swamped with visitors ever since." He was amazed that Sunni hadn't snorted out loud at this speech. Special status! They had that all right, especially with Shug and his cronies, not to mention Soranzo and his spies.

"You're determined to do this, aren't you?" Munro looked disconcerted. "What do you think, Sunni?"

Sunni lifted her chin. "I want to go in with him."

Blaise suppressed a grin. *She's with me on this!*

"I see." Munro crossed his arms over his chest.

"You watch the Oculus and kill its flame when we give you the signal," she said. "If something goes wrong, you can bring help in after us."

"You're very sure of yourselves." Munro strode back to the scattering of matches on the floor and began gathering them into the box.

"Well—" Blaise began.

Munro put his hand up to stop him. Without looking at them, he busied himself tidying the Oculus's table and straightening out chairs with Lexie trotting about at his ankles. After what seemed like ages, he took his watch from his waistcoat and said, "All right. I'm going to time how long you're inside the projection. Ten minutes maximum."

"But—"

"No argument. I'll cut the flame at ten minutes," said Munro. "Now get yourselves into position before I change my mind."

When the projection appeared on the wall, Blaise led Sunni into the Oculus's beam of light. Looking back, he could just make out Munro's shape hovering above the magic lantern.

"It'll feel weird in a minute," he whispered to her. "Weirder than going through the labyrinth."

"It already is…" Her voice faded as his transformation started. The last thing he heard was Munro calling, "No, I've changed my mind!"

But it was too late.

When her transformation began, Sunni's heart pounded so hard she thought it would explode. But in the next moment, the pounding faded and her body was running on some different energy – if she even had a body any more. She floated like this until the drumming of her heart grew stronger and she was aware she had her limbs back again.

When Sunni opened her eyes, everything around her spun and she collapsed to her knees.

"You'll be okay, Sunni." Blaise was already standing unsteadily and reaching down to help her up. "Come on, get up quick."

She wobbled at first as she took in the warm, torchlit world. There was a lot more in this projection than she had been able to see from the Mariner's Chamber. Terracotta-coloured walls stretched high above them into a dark timber ceiling studded with rows of carved golden discs. Filigreed columns of ivory marble lined a grand arched stairway.

A figure in black stood motionless at the top of the stairs. The familiar profile with its dark beard and hooked nose sent a shock of recognition through Sunni.

"Fausto Corvo," she murmured.

"Yes," Blaise said in a low voice. "He was there the last time too, frozen just like that. But watch." He cleared his throat and said loudly, "Signor Corvo. Greetings."

The artist's figure slowly came to life and turned towards them with lowered eyes. He took a deep, but stiff, bow and stayed in that position as he spoke.

"Your Imperial Majesty, welcome to this shadowland." Corvo's accented voice was toneless. "It makes my heart sing that you are here. It means Your Majesty safely received the gift of Fausto Corvo's Oculus and his glass paintings. *Il* Corvo wishes he could greet you himself but he had to flee and hide from the villain Soranzo who covets his secrets. I am *il* Corvo's double, painted and brought to life by his own hand and the power of the heavens. For Your Majesty's pleasure and knowledge, I will act out *il* Corvo's last moments in Venice. If you look carefully you will also find clues in the hunt for the three enchanted paintings he made for you."

The sound of men's voices and the crooning of violins echoed down from the floor above.

"What's that?" Sunni whispered.

"You'll see," Blaise replied. "Stay still."

When Corvo's double spoke again his voice was stronger. "Your Majesty, in a moment you will learn how *il* Corvo escaped Venice in the autumn of 1582 and why he could not wait any longer for your messenger to arrive and transport the enchanted paintings to you." He turned his head slightly as the voices neared, but remained bowed. "Do not be afraid of what you see in this shadowland, Your Majesty. Follow me, then come back to this place and you will return home safely."

The music stopped abruptly and the voices rose. There was a distant sound of rapid footsteps thudding and sliding down unseen steps.

Corvo's double finally straightened up and looked at Sunni and Blaise for the first time. At first his black eyes were blank, then bewildered. Then, with a grim expression, he flew down the uppermost stairs, his long cloak trailing. As he turned onto the landing, he flipped the cloak over one shoulder and leaned across the railing to scan the floor below.

A cluster of men in richly coloured doublets and breeches appeared at the stair head shouting and stamping their feet. The two loudest among them, a short burly young man and a sallow-skinned one with a scarred eyebrow, were at the front of the pack, scolding Corvo's double.

"No one may turn his back on Soranzo like that," the short one called.

The double gripped the hilt of the glinting rapier at his side and said from between gritted teeth, "Go back upstairs, Zago, and tell Soranzo I will have nothing further to do with him."

"How dare you!" the second man yelled. "After the generous offers he has made for your paintings."

"I do not care what he offers, Magno. The three paintings he wants are not for sale. Especially to him!"

Magno responded to this with an elaborate hand gesture of disgust. "You will regret this. My master will not take it lying down."

Corvo's double disdainfully turned on his heel and galloped down the staircase, head held high. As he passed Sunni and Blaise, he gave them another puzzled glance and tore through an arched doorway leading to another hall.

Zago and Magno ran to the stair landing and hung over the railing shouting abuse after him.

"Now, before they get down the stairs!" Blaise clasped Sunni's arm and pulled her across the smooth floor. Rooms and halls flew by in a dizzying blur of fire-lit walls, columns and arches. He guided her past a manservant unconscious on the floor and through a tall half-opened door into a dusky courtyard.

"He said to follow," Blaise whispered. "But where's he gone?"

They passed between two human-sized statues on plinths and emerged into a winding street in time to see a dark shape moving quickly in the distance.

"There he is," she gasped.

"We'll never catch up! Faster!"

"Blaise!" Sunni cried. "We only have ten minutes. Munro's going to pull us back to Blackhope Tower soon."

"So we have to move fast." He sneaked a look around the corner, grabbed her hand and led her down the street, skirting the edges of buildings. The lane opened up into a deserted piazza by a narrow canal. "Where did he go?"

They walked in a circle, peering at the lanes that led away from the piazza.

"He wants us to follow but he leaves us behind? We may as well pick a direction at random," she said, frustrated. "They all look the same."

"This one." Blaise jogged to the next turn and darted into a darkening lane studded with overhanging balconies and wrought iron signs jutting out from decrepit walls. They crept along until the lane was so narrow the houses' roofs nearly touched each other and little sky remained. At last the buildings closed in and the lane became a dead end.

Blaise banged the heel of one hand on a wall. "Oh, great!"

"Yeah, wrong choice." Sunni pulled her wavy hair back to let air onto her damp neck. "It's been more than ten minutes. Munro should have beamed us out by now."

"*Leave the light and travel the shadowlands*," said Blaise, repeating the inscription on the silver box. "Sunni, we're not in the Oculus's *light* any more. Munro can't see us in the projection."

"Does he have to?"

"Corvo's clone said to follow him, then return. We have to be back in the same spot we arrived in." For the first time, he sounded nervous.

"But what if Zago and Magno are hanging about?"

"What choice is there?" Blaise shrugged. "And it looks

like Corvo's double isn't going to show up, so let's go. It's getting dark fast."

They set off at a brisk pace, silent and preoccupied. Sunni's head was lowered, scanning the uneven ground, while Blaise marched a few steps ahead.

"Whose stupid idea was this?" Sunni muttered. "I should have known it would go wrong, just like London."

Blaise's head snapped round. "Oh, right. Are you blaming me?"

"Well, you made it sound so simple. We'll be in and out in ten minutes!" she grumbled.

Blaise didn't answer.

Something dawned on Sunni. "And you knew Corvo's double was there. You saw him when you were in the projection on your own. But you didn't say anything about it."

"That's why I wanted to go back in," he said, stopping short. "But I didn't want to tell you in front of Munro."

Before she could reply, a sweeping black form bolted from the shadows, arms outstretched. With one curling swipe, it pushed Sunni and Blaise together and dragged them backwards. A powerful arm twirled her round and pinned her against a rough wall. She squeezed her eyes tight, feeling the attacker's hand splayed across the base of her neck and hearing his hard breathing. He had Blaise mashed up against her shoulder, held fast.

"Please," Sunni implored in a choked voice. "Let us go."

The hand eased off her neck slightly. The assailant took hold of their shirts and pulled them forwards together. Slowly Sunni opened her eyes to slits and saw a shadowy man in a dark hood and cloak aiming a diabolically sharp rapier at them.

In a low voice Fausto Corvo's double said, "You are not the Emperor. Whoever you are, walk before me, slowly and without noise. If you run, I kill you."

Chapter 8

Blaise didn't dare look round. The one time he'd moved his face towards his shoulder, he'd heard the hiss of the blade cutting the air in warning. The further they walked, down crowded alleys and over bridges, the more he lost hope that Munro would be able to find them, even if he brought help. But Blaise also remembered what two eighteenth-century thieves, Fleet and Sleek, had taught him in London about moving in the dark, counting doorways and squares as they passed. *Left, then right, then another left*, he noted, as they were directed through a maze of streets.

The double gave a low whistle and commanded them to stop in front of a dark building. He whistled again, more insistently this time, and a door opened.

Blaise gaped at the person holding the candle to guide them in. *Marin.* Though it had been months since he'd encountered Corvo's eldest apprentice in Arcadia, the world beneath *The Mariner's Return*, his blood rose as if it had been yesterday. This was the arrogant and deceitful young man Sunni had fancied and he was one of the last people Blaise wanted to run into again.

Wait a minute, Blaise thought as he studied the apprentice's vacant face. *This guy can't be the real Marin. He must be a double too.*

Marin's double watched Blaise and Sunni pass into the building but showed no flicker of recognition. Murmuring something to his master, he herded them up the stairs and through a warren of rooms until they reached a large workshop with tall, shuttered windows, full of easels, tables and painting materials.

At the sight of the room, Sunni covered her mouth in surprise. Blaise recognised it too. The real Fausto Corvo had recreated this workshop as his hiding place in Arcadia.

Corvo's double directed them to sit on two rough stools as he pulled off his cloak and hood and tossed them to his apprentice. He tapped the sharp tip of his rapier into the floor before them. "Who are you?"

"I'm Blaise and this is Sunniva," Blaise said in a wavering voice. "We are friends of Fausto Corvo from the twenty-first century."

The double's face showed no surprise at this extraordinary news but his eyes flicked slightly from right to left as if he were thinking it over. "I do not understand," he said finally and replaced his rapier at his side.

Sunni, who had been watching Marin's double in wonder, said, "We met Fausto Corvo inside his painting, *The Mariner's Return to Arcadia.* At Blackhope Tower in Scotland."

The black eyes flicked again. "I do not know of this place."

Blaise repeated, "We are friends, not enemies."

"You are not the Emperor." From his jacket Corvo's double produced a miniature oval frame containing a painting of a heavy-jawed man with a full brown beard.

"This is His Imperial Majesty. You are not he."

Before the double hid the miniature away, Blaise noticed a line of letters curving over the bearded man's head. *R-U...*

"Who is he?" Sunni asked in a small voice.

Corvo's lookalike ignored her and gave a sharp whistle. Doubles of two younger apprentices, Dolphin and Zorzi, hurried into the workshop, lighting more candles, lanterns and a small fireplace. Loyal and trusted pupils, they quickly gathered sketches from tables and shelves while Corvo and Marin took framed paintings down from the walls, prising the canvases out of their frames and off their wooden supports.

"Sunni," Blaise called under his breath and nodded towards some paintings that hadn't been removed yet. "Look."

She nodded, acknowledging what he had recognised as soon as he saw them – the three magical paintings that all the turmoil was about. They had witnessed the same paintings in Arcadia, protected by the real Fausto Corvo. He, Sunni and Dean had even helped the apprentices fight off Mr Bell's cousin, Angus, to keep him from stealing them. They were much more than beautiful and strange pictures. For under their surfaces Corvo had painted signs and symbols in living painted worlds that contained all his magical knowledge of ancient civilisations. Whoever possessed them could live forever in any of the three wondrous underworlds endowed with the mastery of the universe. But Corvo had meant his three masterpieces for an emperor, not Soranzo or anyone else.

The first painting showed noblemen on horses travelling over a mountainous terrain, towards a distant city with a silver chalice shining in the sky above it. A dead stag lay near them at the foot of a cliff, with scavenger birds assembling above it.

The second painting was a landscape of a vast golden metropolis protected by seven concentric walls and abundant with flowering trees and springs. Each wall was painted with colourful illustrations of stars and planets, animals and plants.

Last was a strange painting of a lavishly dressed man and woman inside a temple with broad columns. The walls were covered with odd symbols and set with stones and jewels.

People have been hurting and killing each other to get hold of these paintings for centuries. And this is where all the fuss started, Blaise thought, *with Corvo and his apprentices getting ready to take the paintings out of Venice in 1582.*

When all the sketches were collected in piles and all the paintings taken from their frames, the apprentices bustled from the room. Corvo's double took the sketches to the fireplace and threw them into the flames. Several fell to the floor and Blaise instinctively jumped up to retrieve them. After a quick glance he held them out, and without a word the double put the drawings straight onto the fire.

Blaise winced as they turned to ash, but the double turned away from the fire with no expression on his face. He rolled the three magical paintings together and put them inside a long leather satchel.

"You do not take your eyes from these three paintings," Corvo's double said, patting the satchel. "You want to steal them for yourself. You think they will teach you to have power over the stars and planets."

"No, we don't want them! We are not Fausto Corvo's

enemies!" Sunni answered, her cheeks red. "No one can ever take those three paintings from him. They're safe forever inside *The Mariner's Return to Arcadia*. We have seen them there with our own eyes."

The double's eyes flicked back and forth again as he thought, sending a strange chill down Blaise's spine.

"Perhaps." He divided the rest of his paintings into two more satchels. In the last one he placed only a roll of unpainted canvas. "I do not know."

He walked around the workshop stuffing small items into a small bag across his chest: sticks of red, ochre and dark brown chalk, bits of parchment and tools.

"Where is Fausto Corvo's Oculus?" the double asked as he gathered things.

"In Blackhope Tower," said Blaise. "A man called Munro owns it now."

Corvo's double stopped and poked the ashes on the glowing hearth. The light played on his dark shape as he turned to face them. "Then the Emperor does not have the shadow lantern. If his Majesty does not have it, he cannot come to this land." He pointed mournfully at the long satchels of paintings. "And he will never learn where Fausto Corvo hid his three enchanted paintings for safekeeping."

"But Corvo *has* them!" Blaise said, at the edge of his seat. "And they are safe, even if the Emperor never got them."

The double began extinguishing lanterns and candles until the air was heavy with smoke and gloom.

"I'm sorry you didn't get to meet the Emperor," Sunni said softly.

Stony-faced, the double pulled on his cloak and a hat,

fastening them securely. He whistled to the apprentices, who filed in wearing capes, hats and small bags across their chests. He strapped a long leather satchel on each boy's back and then his own. Marin's blank-faced double was given the last one with the empty canvas inside.

His face half in shadow, Corvo's double turned to extinguish the last candle. "Get up. We go now, before Soranzo comes," he said to Sunni and Blaise, his hand touching the rapier's hilt. "When we have gone, you will leave this shadowland and never return."

"Yes, sir," said Sunni.

With a swift hand gesture the double sent everyone to the door and snuffed out the last candle. Outside he hastened them under arches and through gates until the dark streets opened onto quays. The moored ships twinkled with lamplight and sailors crawled over them, making ready to sail.

Blaise walked close to Sunni and whispered, "Are you all right?"

"Not really. We're so far away from the Oculus's light now."

He couldn't think of anything that would make her feel better, because she was right. And he'd lost track of how many doorways and squares he'd counted.

"Sir." Blaise broke the silence. "How do we find the way out?"

In a flat voice the double said, "You will be shown." He pulled his hat low over his face and the apprentices did the same. When they reached one ship, he stopped and spoke to a man barking orders at sailors. Blaise noticed the ship's name on its bow and was puzzled at the strange mix of letters that didn't look like any language he'd seen before. The gobbledygook was divided into three words and he could make no sense of them:

VYLNLUG LUVUHOM GUULN

The seaman took a small pouch that Corvo's double gave him and gestured to Zorzi, the youngest lookalike. The boy hung his head as the others wrapped an arm round him in a rapid goodbye. Zorzi trudged up the gangplank and they moved on.

Dolphin watched them from the deck of a smaller ship after the double paid his passage to an unknown destination. The name of his vessel was as unintelligible as Zorzi's:

VYLNLUG LUVUHOM UJLCF

Only Marin did not receive a fatherly embrace from the double. He stood expressionless in the light of a nearby lantern after Corvo gripped his upper arm hard for a second and then strode off. The eldest lookalike stalked onto his ship, whose odd name was also painted on the bow.

VYLNLUG LUVUHOM GYC

Corvo's double made Blaise and Sunni walk along the darker edges of the docks, all the way to the furthest ship that had no name painted on its hull. As they stood in the shadows he said to them, "Leave this place now."

"We don't know the way," Sunni said.

The black eyes stared. "The way will be shown. Go."

She glanced back at the dark contour of the city and sighed. "Okay. Thank you."

The double pulled his long satchel of paintings higher over his shoulder and turned towards the ship.

"Goodbye," said Blaise. He nodded at the satchel. "The enchanted paintings… they *are* safe. I swear."

The man's palm opened briefly, revealing something flat and metallic before he closed his fingers over it. "If the Emperor does not have them, they are not safe. They are still waiting to be found."

Sunni and Blaise watched the double's ship pull away, gliding into the lagoon with its lanterns still shining in the gathering dawn.

"Why would he think the paintings are still out there somewhere?" she asked.

"He doesn't think – he's just a clone with a script. And we weren't part of his script so whatever we said didn't compute," said Blaise, quickly jotting down the odd names of the three apprentices' ships in his sketchbook.

"Maybe," Sunni said slowly. "We saw the three paintings in Arcadia, but…"

"But what?"

"What if they're just copies too, like the ones Corvo's clone packed in his bag?"

"You think that somehow the clone could be right?" he scoffed.

"Well, he made out that Fausto Corvo hid the three paintings for the Emperor to find. And he put clues in these projections."

"Yeah, but we *know* the hiding place is inside *The Mariner's Return to Arcadia* with the real Corvo," said Blaise. "Right?"

"I suppose," said Sunni. "But if that's true, the clone would know too, wouldn't he? So why didn't he recognise *The Mariner's Return to Arcadia* and Blackhope Tower when I mentioned them?"

"Oh." Blaise frowned. "I see what you mean."

"The three magical paintings might still be lost, Blaise! And the clone says the answer is in these projections."

"But how do we find it if he won't help us?"

She sighed. "I don't know."

They were not alone on the quay. From the corner of his eye Blaise saw Zago, watching the double's departing vessel intently.

"Stay still," he hissed. "It's that guy, Zago. The other one might be around too." Alarmed, he scanned the docks, searching for the sallow man with the scarred eyebrow.

"He hasn't noticed us," whispered Sunni.

"Too busy watching Corvo's clone."

As soon as the double's ship was out of sight, Zago melted into the shadows.

"I bet he's heading off to report back to his boss," whispered Blaise.

"Let's go after him."

They followed Zago through the jumble of narrow streets and squares, hiding beside bridges and ducking into doorways as early morning light lit up the city. As he crossed yet another piazza by a canal, Sunni said, "I recognise this place. I think I do, anyway. Venice is confusing."

Blaise's heart leapt. "No, you're right. I remember it too."

"Thank you, Zago!" she muttered as they darted after him. "If we get out of here, do you want to go into the other two slides? I mean, that's what Corvo meant by shadowlands, right? The worlds inside the projections?"

"Yeah," said Blaise. "And yeah."

"I thought you'd say that."

"I've got to find out if the clone is right about the three paintings," he said, keeping a keen eye on Zago as he turned into a lane. "What about you?"

"Yes," she said. "But how are we going to convince

Munro to let us keep going?"

Blaise thought for a moment. "Well, we'll just have to say it again – we're the only ones who can deal with Corvo's magical worlds. I guess we'd have to tell him the basics of what we saw here. But I don't think we should say too much."

"No." Sunni peered into the lane Zago had followed. "Hey, he's just turned the corner again. This is definitely the right way!"

They raced to catch up, tailing Soranzo's spy as he sauntered down the winding street that led to his master's palatial house. Zago walked briskly between the two statues outside and stepped over a servant propped up asleep against the frame of the open door. Blaise held his breath as he and Sunni waited a few moments and did the same.

The rooms were still and dim, and they could hear the slap-slap of Zago's shoes climbing marble stairs.

They tiptoed from room to room, alert for any sounds other than the echo of Zago's steps. When they arrived at the base of the grand staircase, the torch next to the hunting tapestry burned brightly in the otherwise shadowy hall. They nearly skidded on the slick floor in their haste to stand in that light.

As Sunni waved her arms up and down to get Munro's attention, Blaise made a chopping motion that he hoped the spirit photographer would read as 'cut the light'.

"Why is this taking so long? Doesn't he see us?" Sunni asked worriedly. "What if it's morning there too and no one's about?"

"It can't be," he said. "Time hasn't just flown in this world – it's rocketed!"

When the familiar pinpricks of light finally danced before Blaise's eyes, he nearly let out a whoop. He allowed the strange sensations to overtake him and carry him back to the Mariner's Chamber.

He came to with Lexie's whiskers brushing his face and Munro pointing at his pocket watch. "I said ten minutes and you've been gone fifteen!"

Chapter 9

"Blaise, stop pulling my hair," said Sunni as she rolled over on the Mariner's Chamber floor and struggled up to a sitting position. "Ouch!"

Blaise stared at her. He was already on his feet and nowhere near her. "I didn't touch your hair. It's flying around by itself!"

"Oh, no." Sunni batted at the invisible fingers yanking locks of her hair with increasing ferocity. "It's her again!"

"The spirit's being, uh, naughty," said Munro with a frown. "She tried to put the Oculus's flame out while you were in the projection. It's a miracle it stayed lit long enough so I could see you when you got back from exploring." He hurriedly pulled his goggles from a bag under the table and strapped them on. "It's no use. This spirit doesn't want to be seen." He glanced down at his cat, languidly stretching and purring. "Even Lexie isn't detecting her."

The invisible spirit pulled Sunni's hair so hard her head jerked painfully to one side.

"Help me get Sunni to a chair, Blaise." Once she was seated, Munro said, "All right, Sunni. Try this. Take deep breaths and say to yourself, *she cannot hurt me, she cannot hurt me....*"

"But she *is* hurting me!" Sunni huffed.

Munro scanned the air around her head and said, "Spirit, you are clearly angry at Sunni, but she does not know why."

I do know actually, Sunni thought. *Lady Ishbel couldn't stand me when she was alive.*

"Spirit," Munro went on in a soothing voice, "we need to understand what is making you so angry. We want to know what we can do to help put your soul to rest. Can you give us a sign?"

The pulling stopped and Sunni gingerly rubbed her scalp. "Thank you, spirit."

Ahhh. A new whirlwind appeared, whipping round the Mariner's Chamber, blowing everyone's hair and whistling through the seats. It gathered force and circled *The Mariner's Return to Arcadia*, shaking its frame so hard that Sunni was afraid it would fall off the wall.

"The painting?" Munro called out. "Something about the painting, spirit?"

Ahhhh! The frame stopped rattling and, as they watched, two invisible hands pressed so hard on the surface, that they made slight impressions in the canvas.

"Spirit, I don't understand," Munro said.

"Looks like she wants in," said Blaise with a meaningful look at Sunni. "Literally."

The invisible hands pulled away and the Mariner's Chamber was silent and still. Sunni and Blaise quickly examined the painting.

"It's all right," said Blaise. "I don't think she damaged it."

"Good. I think you hit on the answer, Blaise," said Munro, giving them a searching look. "She wants to go inside the painting, like you did. That's curious."

"I'd better not say this too loud," Blaise replied, "but we all know nothing's getting inside that painting again."

"Then she's just going to keep torturing me," said Sunni. *Because I'm the one who dragged her out of her precious Arcadia.*

"By tomorrow she should be gone," Munro said in a low voice. "Once Halloween is over."

"We can't afford for her to mess us about today," Sunni said. "It's really important." She took a deep breath and added, "We need to go into the next slide. Now."

"What?" Munro raked back his slightly ruffled hair. "I'm getting an explanation, right?"

"Sure," said Blaise. "The room Corvo painted in the first slide is in a recreation of Venice. And a clone of him is there – alive and moving around."

Munro beamed. "That's amazing. Go on."

"The projection you saw on the wall just showed a tiny piece of the world Corvo recreated. The rest, which you couldn't see, is called the shadowlands, like in the inscription," said Blaise. "We watched Corvo's clone and his apprentices pack up his paintings and run away from Venice on a ship. It was like a video diary, but we could talk to him."

"You talked to him – and saw his paintings?" Munro was incredulous. "All that in fifteen minutes?"

"Yes, time moves incredibly fast in there," said Sunni, crossing her fingers behind her back for what she was about to say. "And we have to explore the other two slides so we can tell his story to the world. *Just us*, no one else."

Munro's face fell. "I can't go into my own slides? What about the experts in Venice? They'll definitely want to see all this."

Blaise put his hands up. "We'll have to ask Corvo's clone first."

"I'm sorry, but why should you be the only ones allowed in?" Munro asked. "It's a bit odd."

"Not really," said Blaise. "We're the only ones who understand his magical worlds. We told him who we were and, you know, that we're experts like you said..."

Sunni jumped in. "Corvo thinks anyone who comes into the shadowlands is an enemy, trying to find out his secrets. But we seem to be okay."

"Yeah," said Blaise. "He's also got a very sharp sword and he almost used it on us. I'd hate to be a stranger in there..."

"All right, I take your point," said Munro, going over to the Oculus and easing the first slide out of its slot. He held up another with the numeral II etched onto the wooden frame and said, "Here's Corvo's second slide. I'll want to know a lot more about it when you return."

Sunni gave him a subdued smile. "If the spirit lets us."

"Don't you worry about her," said Munro. "I'll keep that flame lit if it's the last thing I do." When the second slide was securely in position, he added a bit of oil to the container and lit the wick.

"Thanks," said Blaise.

Munro checked his pocket watch. "Let's hope this visit doesn't last much longer than the first one. I have another performance in forty-five minutes."

"We'll be back as soon as we can," said Sunni. "Just one thing. We definitely have to be where we started – and the Oculus's flame has to go out at the same time – to be transported back."

“It seems that way,” said Munro. “I’ll be here watching and I’ll kill the flame the minute I see you.”

When the Mariner’s Chamber was dark again, the projection of the second slide appeared. It showed an old wall, a rough patch of floor and part of a wooden chair. Sunni shut her eyes to face the Oculus’s light and within seconds her body tingled and waves of energy flowed through her. She was spun through time and space, disassembled and reassembled perfectly inside the second projection.

Her nose was assaulted by indescribable smells, some sour and human, some made by the oily flames of candles she saw on the wooden tables all around her when she opened her eyes. Rank cloaks and moth-eaten fur hats were strewn around their outlandishly dressed owners who sat motionless on stools and crooked chairs in a cramped tavern. They were unlike any men she had ever seen before, even when she was inside Corvo’s painting the previous winter. Some were missing an eye; some had only one or two teeth in their heads. One wore a beard that was braided from chin to tip and flung over his shoulder while another wore a leather mask that covered the top half of his face.

Sunni found herself leaning against the wall with Blaise beside her. And standing rigid by a nearby table was the figure of Fausto Corvo with his long satchel of paintings slung across his back, staring straight ahead.

Blaise nodded quickly at Sunni and said in an even voice, “Greetings, Signor Corvo.”

The figure stirred and bent into a low bow. "Welcome to this shadow-land, Your Imperial Majesty. It makes my heart glad that you are here. It means Your Majesty safely received the gift of Fausto Corvo's Oculus and his glass paintings. *Il* Corvo wishes he could greet you himself but he had to flee and hide from the villain Soranzo who covets his secrets. I am *il* Corvo's double, painted and brought to life by his own hand and the power of the heavens. For Your Majesty's pleasure and knowledge, I will act out *il* Corvo's arrival in your beloved home, Prague, in the winter of 1582. If you look carefully you will also find clues in the hunt for the three enchanted paintings he made for you."

One by one the men around them came to life, resuming conversations in a jumble of languages and drinking from their mugs.

Corvo's double continued. "Your Majesty, in a moment you will learn how *il* Corvo travelled alone from Venice to Prague over many days, hoping to deliver three enchanted paintings to you. Do not be afraid of what you see in this shadowland, Your Majesty. Follow me, then come back to this place and you will return home safely."

"Uh, thank you," Sunni said hastily. "We are not the Emperor but we are friends. We do not want Fausto Corvo's paintings. We want to help protect them."

The double straightened and his eyes flicked back and forth.

"Come on," Blaise muttered to Sunni. He pushed his way onto a stool at the table and motioned for her to join him. She plonked herself onto a chair beside him and looked expectantly at the double.

Before he could speak, a man with skin like wrinkled paper sidled up to the double's side. In his palm was a tiny bird's skeleton in a glass bottle. But all Sunni noticed were the man's hideous fingernails. They were so long they had become monstrous yellow curling claws.

"You are new here, sir," the man said to the double. "See my phoenix relic. A gift for you at a special price."

Corvo's double nudged him away and sat down, never taking his perplexed eyes from Sunni and Blaise. "No, I do not want it."

Another man pressed forwards and offered him a mummified human ear in a small jewelled case, while a third spread out a cloth and dropped crystals of varying sizes upon it. Sunni was slightly nauseated as they leaned in closer with their fetid breath and crazy eyes.

"Surely you must desire something, sir," the first man wheedled.

A ratlike man fanned out a deck of strange playing cards. Another slid a small sketch onto the table and Blaise peered at it with a look of puzzlement. Two more men came up behind Corvo's double, sharp and predatory. Soon a dozen men were crowded round the table, thrusting trinkets and amulets at him, and many more stood behind.

"No, put away your rubbish," the double said. "I seek information."

The men murmured.

"I wish to deliver something to His Imperial Majesty Rudolf," he said. "I must speak with him in person."

"Oh ho, in person!" someone guffawed. "You will be lucky to get past the palace guards."

"That is," said another, "if they let you cross the Stone Bridge to get to the palace!"

Corvo's double said, "When I tell them how important and precious my delivery is, they will give way."

A few laughed knowingly.

"We've all thought that before," said the man with the crystals. "Who sent you?"

"No one," said the double. "But Emperor Rudolf is expecting my gift."

"So you have papers to prove it," he replied. "Or a letter to introduce you."

"No. I did not expect to be delivering the gift myself."

"Good luck then," the crystal seller smirked, folding up his wares. "You are just another of many men with gifts for the Emperor. Go and join the queue if you don't mind waiting weeks or even months."

One by one the dealers withdrew from the table.

Blaise whispered to the trader who had put the sketch on the table, "Where did you get this?"

The man ignored him.

"Who made it?" Blaise insisted, noticing that Corvo's double was now watching him closely.

But the trader swiped the sketch away and vanished into the crowd. Only one hawker remained at the table, close by the double's side.

"From a centaur," the man said, holding up the mummified ear. "It will cure leprosy."

"Take it away from me," the double said, not noticing the hawker's other hand creeping under his black cloak.

Sunni jumped up. "Watch out!"

Corvo's double caught the man's wrist and squeezed until he dropped a small brass-coloured disc. Before the double hid it again, Sunni recognised it as the object she had seen glinting in the clone's hand on the quay. She had no idea what it was, with its letters engraved round the edge and a red stone at its centre.

"Thief!" Corvo's double pushed the man away and tugged his long satchel close. As he turned to leave, a man in a tattered velvet hat pressed a scrap of paper into his hand.

"This will show you the way to the castle, my friend," he said in a low voice and bustled back into the crowd.

With a curt nod, the double pushed through the tavern. Sunni and Blaise hurried after him, ducking out through a low door into a cold dusk.

When the door had banged shut, the double commanded, "Go back inside and leave this shadowland. You are trespassers."

"We only want to help protect Corvo's paintings. We think they are safe," said Blaise. "We met Fausto Corvo inside *The Mariner's Return to Arcadia* and saw the three enchanted paintings there with him."

The double's eyes had a faraway look as they flicked back and forth.

"You must know the other enchanted painting, *The Mariner's Return to Arcadia*," said Sunni hopefully. "It's in Blackhope Tower where Sir Innes Blackhope once lived."

After a moment he answered, "I do not."

She searched his face for a sign that he was lying but it showed no expression.

"But you do know where Fausto Corvo hid the enchanted paintings?" Blaise asked.

"Yes," said the double. "But that is only for the Emperor to know and you are not he."

"So you're saying the paintings *aren't* inside *The Mariner's Return*."

"I say nothing to anyone but His Imperial Majesty." The black eyes narrowed as he pulled his cloak back to reveal the rapier. "Leave now or you will feel the blade."

Blaise swiftly opened the tavern door and pulled Sunni inside. After a few seconds' wait they dashed outside again. The double was hurrying away along the dim cobbled street, studying the paper scrap and checking people and doorways he passed.

"Sorry, clone," said Sunni, breathing out frosty clouds. "I'm not going home yet."

"Me neither, but just one thing." Blaise pointed at the rotting sign that hung over the tavern entrance. The name was in a language she could not make out, but she knew the mythical creature with the cockerel's head whose long lizard tail wound around the letters.

"A basilisk," she said. "We'd better remember that because we'll need to get back here. Don't know what that name is though."

Blaise stared up at the letters, looking puzzled. "How can that be?" he asked slowly.

"Come on or we'll lose the clone." She rubbed her chilly arms and set off. "We can look at it later."

Prague stank even in the cold. Rotting food, animal manure and worse, the smell had not been masked by the shreds of hard frost that lingered at the corners of the ramshackle houses. The sun had gone in, if it had even been out that day, and the crooked lanes were bathed in an icy blue light.

"The clone knows where the paintings are hidden," Sunni said, her teeth chattering. "And they're not in Arcadia."

"Or he's lying."

"I just don't know any more," she answered.

Panting and shivering, they chased after the double. They crossed a huge square dominated by two lofty church spires at one end and a tower at the other. The air was suddenly filled with the distant sound of bells tolling five. Two high windows opened in the grey tower and a succession of carved figures moved across them to the peal of a golden bell. Below this odd spectacle was an elaborate clock with a small dial within a large one, decorated with astrological symbols and markings around the edges.

Corvo's double veered out of the square and through another tangle of streets until he came to a wide river and a monumental arched bridge with a stone tower at each end.

Beyond it was a hill crowned by a huge castle, majestic and icy-looking, its spires sharp in the frigid indigo sky.

The double paid a toll collector at the stone tower and darted onto the bridge.

"Now what?" muttered Blaise. "We don't have the right money."

"Look!" Sunni pointed through the stone tower's archway, where she could make out the double, half-lit by a nearby torch.

Corvo's double was slowly walking backwards, his rapier raised. Two men loomed before him, one in a mask covering the top half of his face.

"The one in the mask," said Sunni. "He was in the tavern!"

"It's Soranzo's spies, Zago and Magno."

Suddenly Zago pounced and the double knocked him to the ground. Before Magno could put a hand on him, he sheathed his rapier, bolted away to the side of the bridge and climbed onto the stone wall. He pulled the long satchel off his own back and, with a low cry, flung it over the side. Then, to Sunni and Blaise's horror, Corvo's double threw himself into the icy river, his cloak flapping at his back like a pair of raven's wings.

Chapter 10

"Let's get out of here!" Blaise put his arm around Sunni's chilly shoulders. They briskly walked away from the bridge where Soranzo's two spies had hung over the wall, shouting and staring into the black water before they ran off into the night.

"That was horrible," Sunni murmured as they navigated the alleys and into the huge square they'd passed through before.

"Yeah," said Blaise. "Corvo went through a lot to protect those three paintings. Hope it was worth all the trouble."

Prague's church bells tolled seven and again the two dim windows in the strange clock popped open, revealing the carved figures moving across, lit from behind by lanterns.

"It's already seven o'clock?" Sunni asked, gawping at it over her shoulder.

"Time flies when you're having fun."

They picked their way down the shadowy lanes until they found the tavern with the basilisk sign. Blaise stared at the lettering once again.

"Hang on a minute." He fished his small sketchbook from his pocket and showed her a page inside it. "I thought I'd seen that gobbledygook before. It's the same as one of the ships in Venice."

VYLNLUG LUVUHOM GUULN

"That's odd," said Sunni. "Unless it's a message. The clone said there were clues for the Emperor in the shadowlands."

Blaise put away the sketchbook. "Maybe it's a code. But we need a way to break it."

"And the clone isn't ever going to tell us," said Sunni. "because we're not the Emperor."

She pulled the tavern door open. The tavern was teeming and even more rancid-smelling, which may have had something to do with the various exotic animals and birds being carried around by smiling dealers. As he was taller than most, Blaise came face to face with a shivering monkey and a solemn parrot whose cages were being paraded above their owners' heads.

Sunni was at his side, then pushing ahead of him. Someone yanked his arm, pointing towards a table covered in animal horns and shouting about unicorns. A hand was feeling around his waist, sliding towards his pockets.

"Whoa!" He slapped the hand away. "Oh, no, you don't!"

"Go on, Blaise!" Sunni was now pulling his elbow and shouting at the people pressing in on them.

"Out of my way!" With his hands shoved into his pockets to ward off the thieves, Blaise waded through the throng, kicking stools out of the way. He practically hurled himself towards the wall where Sunni and he had first appeared. She was already there, waving her arms to get Munro's attention back at the Mariner's Chamber.

"Munro!" he yelled. "Get us out of here now!"

"*What* is going on?" asked Lorimer Bell.

Blaise was still shaking when, after a sharp knock, their art teacher unlocked the Mariner's Chamber door with his key and switched the overhead light on.

Sunni was on the floor too, looking like she'd been dropped there, while a surprised Munro batted away a curl of smoke rising from the Oculus.

Lorimer shut the chamber door firmly behind him, his eyebrows knitted together. "Blaise! Sunniva."

"Mr B." Blaise couldn't remember the last time Lorimer had called her Sunniva, and he saw her wince as she got up.

"Munro?" Lorimer turned to the spirit photographer. "What's going on here?"

"They were just doing a bit of an experiment with the projection from this magic lantern," said Munro. "It's all absolutely fine, Lorimer."

"What, making shadows with their hands or something?" Lorimer asked. "How did they end up on the floor?"

Blaise rolled over and got to his feet, still slightly unsteady. "We just lost our balance, Mr B."

"Lost your balance doing *what*?" Lorimer looked pointedly at his pupil.

Blaise brushed some dust off his shirt and jeans and gave Sunni a sidelong glance. "It's a little complicated."

The art teacher looked at his watch. "I've got time. Let's hear it."

Blaise shot Sunni a glance and she nodded. There was

no way they could keep this from him. "Well, first off, this isn't Munro's fault."

The spirit photographer gave them a grim smile.

"We convinced him to let us try it," said Sunni. "And it worked."

"For heaven's sake," said Lorimer. "Try what?"

"Going into the projections," she said brightly. "We've gone into Fausto Corvo's painted slide projections. Each one is a different world..."

Lorimer stared at them in disbelief. "You've been able to come and go into projections on a wall?"

They nodded.

"We found out how to do it by accident. I just stepped into the Oculus's light," said Blaise. "It feels funny and it takes a few seconds to feel your normal self afterwards, but it works."

"And you stood by and let them do this?" Lorimer turned on Munro, incredulous. "Do you have any idea what these two went through last winter in this very room?"

"Yes, I know." Munro's face fell. "I didn't think it was a good idea at first but they insisted. And, look, they're back fit and well!"

"We're okay, I swear," Blaise said. "And it's not the same as being inside *The Mariner's Return to Arcadia*. You can get in and out much more easily."

Lorimer crossed his arms over his chest. "I'm not happy about this, Blaise."

"But we even had a back-up plan," he replied. "If we didn't get back in a certain amount of time, Munro could come after us with help."

"Which I didn't need to do," said Munro with a slightly injured air. "Because it's all *fine*."

"Well, Munro," sniffed Lorimer. "It's not all fine in the Mysteries and Curiosities marquee. Aurora sent me to find you because people have been asking for you. You really should be down there between your Oculus shows."

"Oh right, sorry." Munro looked at his pocket watch. "Tell Aurora I'll pop by later."

"No." Lorimer frowned. "You can go and tell her yourself. If you don't mind."

"I need to be here—"

"You've got time before your next show. I'll lock the door after I've had a chat with my pupils," said the art teacher.

Munro reluctantly picked up his top hat and patted it onto his head. "Don't let anyone touch the Oculus," he warned.

"I don't intend to," said Lorimer. "Goodbye, Munro."

The spirit photographer gave Sunni and Blaise a wink as he left with Lexie in his arms.

"All right," said Lorimer, sitting in one of the chairs. "Explanation please."

Sunni took a breath. "Corvo painted three glass slides for the Oculus," she said. "They look ordinary if you project them on a wall, but if you go inside them you see the story of where he went after he ran away from Soranzo in 1582."

Lorimer's jaw dropped. "Why would he do that?"

"To send a message to someone important." Blaise picked up the third slide from the wooden table and handed it to his teacher. "The Oculus and these slides were meant for an emperor called Rudolf in Corvo's time."

“So were his three lost magical paintings. They were going to be gifts,” added Sunni, as Lorimer held the slide up to the overhead light. Blaise noticed she was looking over her shoulder and brushing something away with her fingers.

“But we don’t think they ever made it to the Emperor.” Blaise took the slide back and laid it carefully next to the Oculus. “They’ve been lost for centuries.”

“You told me you’d seen them with Corvo when you were in Arcadia last winter,” said Lorimer.

“We did,” said Blaise. “But now we’re not so sure.”

Sunni jumped in. “The Emperor was supposed to receive the Oculus and the slides and go inside each projection like we just did. There’s a clone of Corvo in each one, put there to tell the Emperor where the paintings are. And the clone told us the Emperor never showed up. He thinks the paintings are still out there somewhere.”

“Wait,” said Lorimer, shaking his head. “A clone of Corvo talked to you?”

“Yes,” she said, twitching her shoulders and frowning. “I know that sounds weird. The projections are like a video diary with the clone acting out Corvo’s story.”

“This is too much.” Their teacher let out a long breath. “Astonishing.”

“All the real Corvo wanted to do was protect his three magical paintings,” said Blaise. “And we’ve got to help him do that.”

“So you want to keep hunting for them?” asked Lorimer.

“Yes,” said Sunni, still fidgeting. “We hope we’ll find the answer in the last projection.”

They all fell silent.

"Sunni, Blaise." Lorimer pressed his palms together. "This is huge. I can imagine how excited you are. But I can't let you go inside again."

"But Mr B!" Blaise screwed up his face. "Munro let us go and he owns the Oculus."

"Yes, but he's a guest on Blackhope Tower property and he should know better."

"Nothing happened to us," Sunni cried out.

"Your flesh and bones were transported – by Corvo's sorcery – into a light projection. I can't even begin to imagine what that might have done to your systems," said Lorimer, his voice rising. "And I'll bet your parents haven't a clue what you've been doing."

Blaise gave Sunni a look. "This isn't fair, Mr B. We're old enough to look after ourselves."

"Not quite," said Lorimer.

"We've got to go into the third projection." Blaise's face clouded with anger and disappointment.

"No, Blaise, and that's final." Lorimer ran his hand over his shaved head. "I think you should both go home now."

"But we can't just leave it like this, Mr Bell!" Blaise exclaimed.

"I'll talk to Munro," said Lorimer. "You've told him everything you told me?"

"We didn't have time," said Sunni, her mouth drooping. "He knows Corvo's clone was in the first projection. That's all."

"Fine," said the teacher. "I'll sort it out."

"But you don't understand," Blaise murmured under his breath.

Lorimer let out an exasperated breath. "Come on, time to go, guys. You've been here long enough and I must be getting on."

Blaise picked up a stray wick from the floor and placed it next to the Oculus, eyeing the magic lantern longingly.

Sunni was halfway to the door when she paused and turned to her teacher. "You're not going to tell our parents about this, are you, Mr Bell?"

"If you're both sure you're all right, no, I don't have to mention it. But if you feel any adverse effects later on, they'll have to know what you got up to. Whether they'll believe it or not, I don't know."

"I could take my dad into the projection," muttered Blaise, "and prove it!"

"You're not going back in, with your dad or anyone else," said Lorimer, herding them to the door. "This whole thing is one of Corvo's secrets and it's best to keep it that way for now."

"Thanks, Mr B,' said Sunni.

"Yeah," said Blaise. "Thanks a *lot*."

Lorimer gave them a strained smile. When they were a few metres down the corridor, Blaise turned and caught a glimpse of the teacher's back, his fingers scraping nervously at his neck, before he heard the Mariner's Chamber door slam shut.

Chapter 11

Blaise was still fuming as he and Sunni crossed Blackhope Tower's entrance hall.

"I feel so ripped off," he said in a low voice. "If only Mr Bell hadn't come in."

"I know," said Sunni.

"We've got to talk to Munro before he does."

"I bet Munro won't have anything to do with us now," said Sunni. "It's over, Blaise. We won't get another chance at the last projection." She twisted round and tried to see the back of her trousers. "My back pocket got ripped by one of those weirdos in the tavern. Does it look really obvious?"

"Nope, I don't think so," he answered.

She tried to smooth her hair down. "Do I look semi-normal?"

"Yes, you look semi-normal."

"Rhona doesn't miss anything so I'd better keep my back to the wall when I go home." She pushed the main door open and a gust of wind swept her wavy hair up over her face. "Oh, wonderful."

The sun had vanished, giving way to grey clouds scudding across the sky. Most festival visitors had sought refuge inside the heated marquees or the castle, except for a few who braved the chilly breeze.

"Blaise!" A shout came from the entrance to the food tent, where Iona stood sipping from a plastic cup. "Over here!"

"Hey." He strode over to her side. "How're you doing?"

"Fabulous." She stroked one of the skeleton-shaped earrings she wore. "Where did you get to last night?"

"I looked around and then I had to head home. Did you get the Great Hall decorations finished?"

"Oh, yes," she drawled. "It looks amazing, if I say so myself."

Sunni appeared at his side, still trying to keep the flying hair from her face. "Hello."

"Hiya," said Iona casually. "So are you coming to the fancy dress party tonight, Blaise?"

"I doubt it," said Blaise.

"We'll be there," said Iona. "Wouldn't miss it."

Blaise could tell by the way Sunni stood so stiffly that she was not happy. "Iona, you know Sunni, right? Sunni, this is Iona."

"Hi," said Sunni tonelessly.

"Sure." Iona gave her a sweet smile.

"How you doing, Blaise?" asked James, looming up behind Iona and tousling her sleek copper hair.

"Good, yeah," he answered.

"Some mad people in there," said James, jerking his thumb at the Mysteries and Curiosities tent. "Phew."

"Aurora's my favourite," said Iona. "She's wired to the moon, but lovely."

Munro walked past with Lexie cradled in his arms, deep in conversation with someone. The cat eyed them but her owner seemed not to have noticed them at all and Blaise's heart sank. Sunni was right. He probably wouldn't want anything to do with them now.

"Speaking of mad," James said under his breath. "Munro's another one. Have you seen his transport? It's an old hearse."

"That cat's just as bonkers," said Iona.

"And his photos are totally spooky," James said approvingly. "They look like normal pictures but there's always something off about them and you aren't sure what it is at first. And then you notice a face in the background that shouldn't be there, or a hand floating in mid-air."

"I've got to go," Sunni said from somewhere just behind Blaise.

"Yeah, me too." He shook himself into action. "Catch you later."

"Wait." Iona tapped something into her phone and showed it to him. "That's my number. If you change your mind, James or I can leave you tickets at the door."

Blaise fumbled with his phone and punched her number in.

"Now call me so I have yours," said Iona. When her phone buzzed a moment later she announced, "Done. See you."

"Maybe later," called James.

"Thanks. Bye." Blaise scurried after Sunni. "Hey, wait up."

"Stay with your new pals if you want," she said when he caught up, and then began muttering something under her breath.

"I hardly know them. I was being polite," he said, catching her by the elbow. "What's the problem?"

"Ever since we got out of the projection I've had Lady Ishbel picking at my clothes and whooshing round my ears!" she exploded. "I think she wants to drive me crazy. If only I could get her back into Arcadia so she'd leave me alone."

"Why didn't you say?"

"I'm trying to ignore her, like Munro said, but it's impossible in the Mariner's Chamber. She's really strong there."

"Maybe because that's where she died. How are things now?"

"Better. I don't think I've shaken her though. She seems to come and go."

"Sorry, Sunni."

"I just want to get home."

They walked through the swaying trees along the old Blackhope Road that meandered into town. Blaise knew Sunni preferred this because fewer cars drove this way and there would be less chance her stepmother would see her. One day he was going to challenge Rhona and find out what was so bad about Sunni being with him, but not today.

Right now, all he wanted to do was get home and figure out what he could do about Corvo's last slide – if there *was* anything he could do.

"What are you up to tonight?" Sunni asked.

"I don't know. Nothing." Blaise felt a sudden niggle of displeasure. "We might have been in and out of the last projection by now." He kicked away a clump of leaves that blew against his leg.

"Let it go," said Sunni. At the crossroads before the Wee Cuppa Café, she gave him a tired smile and turned to go into her street. "What a day. I'm knackered actually."

"I'm not," said Blaise. "I'm wired." He sighed. "We came so close."

Sunni shrugged. "Give it a rest."

"Have a good night, Sunni," he said softly.

"You, too." She walked away slowly, as if she were carrying a burden, with locks of her hair still blowing up even though the wind had died down.

A razor-thin chill ran down Blaise's neck as he watched her. He didn't need a cat or goggles to know that Lady Ishbel was getting to Sunni and there was nothing they could do about it.

It was dark when Sunni woke from her nap. She could smell food cooking and she knew it must be close to teatime. She was getting out of bed, relieved at how much brighter she felt, when her phone rang.

"Sunni?" Blaise sounded breathless on the other end. "How're you doing?"

"All right. What's up?"

"Something's happened." He was jumpy. "I'm going to the fancy dress party at Blackhope Tower. Can you come?"

A thrill ran through her. "Okay."

"What about Ishbel? Are you up for dealing with her?" he asked.

"Yeah, if I have to."

"Can you get out of the house?"

"I'll find a way. What's going on?"

Blaise lowered his voice. "It's not good."

"Tell me."

"I can't. Look, the party doesn't start until later, but we have to go soon. Can you meet me back at the old Blackhope Road in half an hour?"

Sunni only hesitated for a couple of seconds. "Yes. I'll be in a ghost maiden costume. Just so I don't freak you out."

Blaise cursed. "Oh man, I still have to find a costume!"

"Just wear anything. It doesn't matter."

"My dad might have something. See you in half an hour." He hung up abruptly.

Sunni sprang into action, pulling on her white wig and gown and applying her pale make-up in record time. Her mind was occupied with concocting the best story she could because it was going to have to be convincing.

She presented herself in the kitchen, where Rhona and her dad were dishing up supper and calling for Dean to come down.

"Well, well, well," said her dad. "You've gone all pale and interesting, sweetheart. Who are you meant to be?"

"Just a ghostly maiden." Sunni adopted her best girly excited voice. "I've been invited to the fancy dress party tonight at the Enigma Festival."

"Really?" Rhona had her suspicious face on. "Who by?"

"James." She almost faltered. "James Ross."

"The James Ross whose photo was in the *Evening*

Sentinel the other week?" Rhona's eyebrows rose. "Whose father is a doctor?"

"Yeah."

Rhona gave Sunni's dad an approving smile. "Well, Sunni, this is a bit of a surprise. You haven't said anything about him before."

"I haven't known him that long." She squeezed two fingers together into a cross behind her back, even though everything she'd said was true, sort of. It was more about what she'd left out.

"Is James picking you up here? We'd like to meet him," said her dad.

"Um, no. I'm meeting him and some other kids from school." She beamed them a hopeful smile. "In ten minutes."

"We're about to eat. You can't go out on an empty stomach."

"There's going to be food at the party, Dad," Sunni wheedled. "Please?"

Rhona gave him a knowing look and said, "Maybe we can make an exception this time, Ian, don't you think?"

"Well, I suppose. Will this boy be bringing you home, by the way?" her dad asked.

"Of course. I'll be fine, Dad." She heard Dean clumping down the stairs. "But it might be a bit late."

"You know when you're supposed to be in," he replied firmly, but smiled.

Dean plunked himself down at the table. He wore a ripped striped shirt with a leather vest over it and a black patch over one eye. A pirate hat was perched jauntily on his blonde head.

"You going out?" Sunni asked.

"Yeah. Halloween party." He drummed the table with his fork and spoon. "Where are you going, ghoul girl?"

Rhona winked at Sunni in a girl-to-girl kind of way that nearly made Sunni faint with surprise. Going on a fake date with James was the first thing she'd ever done that her stepmother seemed excited about.

"She's going to the fancy dress party at Blackhope Tower, Dean. And you can't wear that awful jacket, Sunni." Rhona vanished into the hall cupboard and came back with her own long knitted white cardigan. "This is more ghostly looking and quite warm. Just keep it clean please."

Still in shock at being lent one of her stepmother's things, Sunni pulled it on and made for the back door. "Thanks, Rhona. This is amazing."

She hurried to the crossroads and the dark turn into the old Blackhope Road, where a lanky figure stood in a long tatty cape. Blaise swung round and finished a phone conversation when he saw her approaching.

"Wow. You look…" His voice trailed off.

"Ghostly?" she volunteered.

"Beautiful," he murmured. "You look beautiful."

They stood still with the breeze swirling round them. Sunni waited, her heart thumping. *He said I'm beautiful.* It didn't matter that she had white hair and white lips and sooty smudges around her eyes. *He said I'm beautiful.*

But Blaise didn't move from the spot. He seemed to be holding his breath and just smiled stupidly.

Come on, Blaise. Don't stop there. When she twigged that he had frozen and wasn't about to unfreeze, Sunni asked in a hushed voice, "What's so urgent?"

His face suddenly changed from gormless to serious. "That was Iona on the phone again. No one can find Mr Bell."

Chapter 12

Sunni stopped by the entrance to a path marked by a crooked tree.

"You want to cut through the woods instead?" she asked.

Blaise squinted uncertainly into the dark. "No, let's stick to the road. What did you tell your parents?"

"Don't ask," said Sunni. "Now what's going on?"

He followed her pale figure along the footpath, dead leaves crunching underfoot and his mildewed velveteen cape swishing as they walked. Every so often he looked back to make sure no one was following them.

"Iona called me and asked when I last saw Mr Bell. I told her and said to call me back if they didn't find him," he answered. "And I had this funny feeling they weren't going to."

"And she just phoned you back."

"Yup. No one has seen Mr B since he went to find Munro for Aurora."

"So we're the last people who saw him," said Sunni. "But he was right behind us, wasn't he, when we left the Mariner's Chamber?"

"I don't know," Blaise said. "I heard the door slam but I didn't see him leave."

"Me neither. And that was hours ago."

"Yeah," he said. "So I told Iona we'd head over to Blackhope Tower."

Cars' headlamps flashed across Sunni's white dress as they drove past, and even in the darkness she almost glowed under a fine crescent moon. With the woods beside them crackling and creaking with the wind, and the hint of wood smoke in the air, Blaise could believe that Lady Ishbel's wasn't the only spirit let loose in Braeside.

His thoughts swung back and forth between Sunni and Corvo and Mr Bell. Once again he'd blown it with Sunni. Blaise cringed as he imagined what she'd thought when he'd said she looked beautiful – not as she normally was, but when she was dressed up as a dead girl. *Nice.*

If he wasn't such an idiot, he could have added something like *you're beautiful all the time* and stepped forward, suavely, to envelop Sunni with his cape like Dracula. No, she probably would have squirmed away, wanting to know what he was playing at. Blaise sighed. Just as well he hadn't made any moves then.

"I meant to tell you," he said at last. "While I was home I looked up the Emperor Rudolf who was living in Prague in 1582."

"And?"

"He was called Holy Roman Emperor Rudolf II. And get this. He collected tons of art and weird curiosities from all over the world but he didn't like to travel. So people either brought him treasures or he sent out scouts to find paintings for him."

"That fits," said Sunni. "The clone said Corvo couldn't wait any longer for the Emperor's delivery guy to come and get the three paintings so he took them to Prague himself."

"And something else," said Blaise. "Rudolf was totally into magic and alchemy and was looking for the secret of eternal life."

"So he would have really wanted Corvo's magical paintings," she said.

"Yeah, but he never got them. And it looks like he never received the Oculus either."

The old Blackhope Road wound round and brought them out a short distance from the main road and the entrance to the castle. The lions at the gate were specially illuminated from underneath, making them look as if they were ready to leap off their plinths, and the long drive was dotted with jack o' lanterns grinning into the night.

Two torches burned like beacons on either side of Blackhope Tower's entrance and every window in the castle was lit. Blaise had never seen it looking so grand, as if horses and carriages ought to be pulling up outside.

Inside, the atmosphere was tense. Aurora Midnight, dressed in a floating, moss-coloured fairy queen outfit, was pacing back and forth across the entrance hall clutching a phone to her chest. James burst from the spiral staircase dressed in a tuxedo and his purple paws, carrying his furry headpiece under one arm. Iona, in a glamorous witch costume, and several other pixies, punks and ghouls milled about at the front desk.

"He's not in the gents, either," said James, catching Blaise and Sunni from the corner of his eye and nodding. "I've looked everywhere – again."

"I told you, he's not here," said Iona.

"Did you hear his two-way radio crackling at all?" asked Jimmy, the security guard, scowling. "I was calling him again just now."

"No," said James. "Not a sound."

"Well then," Jimmy said. "He's probably just gone off to get ready for tonight."

"He didn't say anything to me about leaving," said Aurora, her eyes wide.

"Maybe he forgot," Iona said.

"That's not like him." Aurora held up her phone. "This is the umpteenth time I've rung Lorimer and it just clicks dead on the other end. When was the last time any of you saw him? I know I've already asked you, but think again."

Iona rolled her eyes. "I can't remember."

"Sometime this afternoon," James said. "Don't know when."

"I asked him to find Munro for me at about four o'clock." Aurora blinked her green-lidded eyes. "And he didn't come back. None of you saw him after that?"

Sunni spoke up. "We did. In the Mariner's Chamber, about four-fifteen."

"Really?" Aurora asked hopefully. "What happened?"

"We said goodbye and left him there," said Blaise. "He went back to lock the door for Munro."

"And I checked the Mariner's Chamber at five-thirty," said Jimmy. "Munro had just finished his last show of the afternoon and he hadn't seen Mr Bell since he left you two talking to him."

Blaise gave Sunni a furtive glance. "Is Munro around?"

"No," said the security guard. "He left some time ago."

"Look," said Iona. "Mr Bell will turn up for the party. After all the work we did, he's not about to miss that." She straightened her pointed hat. "Come on, James, we've got to fix some bits of my spider web."

As a few bursts from fiddles and bagpipes floated down from the Great Hall, the mob of costumed teenagers brightened up and scurried upstairs, leaving Aurora staring dejectedly at her phone.

"What do you want to do now, Blaise?" Sunni asked, watching the other kids scatter.

Blaise was sniffing his cape. "Does this smell bad to you?"

"Kind of," she said.

Aurora looked over at them with interest and he thought, *Oh no, don't want to get caught up with her*. He pulled the cape off and mashed it into a ball. "There's a bin outside."

"Then you'll have no costume."

"Like you said before, it doesn't matter." He strode down a gravel path towards the nearby stone cottage that had been converted into a gift shop. In one move he slam-dunked the cape into a large bin. "Why didn't you tell me it stank?"

"You needed someone to tell you?"

He swiped the deerstalker from his head. "This is rancid too."

"Okay, are you done?" she asked. "I'd like to know the plan."

"I guess we go to the party and see if Munro shows up," he grumbled.

"And Mr Bell."

"I doubt that," said Blaise. "Sunni, look."

A flickering light caught his eye. It was moving steadily through the trees behind the cottage. After a moment a bizarre shape in a long coat came towards them, its gauntlet-clad hand carrying a hurricane lantern in one hand and a cat in the other. The light played upon the tall stovepipe hat and strange spectacles with frames made from gears and bits of clockwork.

"Munro!" Blaise felt a rush of relief. "Why are you out here?"

"Blaise, Sunni." The spirit photographer recoiled slightly. "You gave me a start. For a moment I thought a couple of new spirits were presenting themselves. Very convincing outfit, Sunni. What about you, Blaise? No costume?"

"It was bad so I dumped it," said Blaise. "But we're really here because we heard Mr Bell's missing."

"Yes," Munro said grimly. "I've been wracking my brains about what to do. I think Lorimer went into the third projection but I can't be sure. When I came back to the Mariner's Chamber to do my next show, the door was locked and the room was dark, as I'd expect. But when I went to put my first slide into the Oculus, Corvo's third slide was already in the slot and the wick was burned out."

"We didn't touch the Oculus," said Sunni.

Munro's lips were set in a line. "You're certain."

"One hundred per cent," said Blaise.

"Then Lorimer used the Oculus when he was alone," said Munro. "I should have told the security people hours ago but I just wasn't sure. This looks very bad."

"What time is your Halloween show tonight?" Blaise asked, his mind racing.

"At nine."

"Then there's time to get Mr Bell out now. He can turn up at the fancy dress party and no one ever needs to know about the Oculus."

Munro gave him a half-smile. "I take it you want to be on the rescue team."

"Yeah," said Blaise. "If you'll let us after this afternoon."

"It would be pretty insane of me," said the photographer, "and I should be the one who goes in. But I wouldn't have a clue what I was doing – and you do."

Blaise grinned. "Let's go then."

"Hold on. What about you, Sunni?" Munro asked. "I'm worried about your spirit companion making mischief."

"I know she's about, but I'm trying to resist her. And she doesn't seem to be able to follow me into the projections." Sunni glanced over her shoulder. "I'll go into the third slide with Blaise."

"All right," said Munro with a resigned sigh. "Look, Blaise, do you want to borrow something for a Halloween costume so you don't stand out?" He turned back towards the woods. "I can lend you a thing or two."

"Okay, why not?"

They followed the path to a dark clearing containing a tent and an ancient hearse with blacked-out windows.

"Home, sweet home." Munro set Lexie on the vehicle's roof and pulled out some folded clothes. "This will probably fit you."

Two minutes later Blaise emerged from behind a tree,

dressed in a burgundy shirt with billowing sleeves and huge cuffs, and adjusting a black eye mask. He pulled a leather belt studded with silver discs and a large buckle through his own black trousers. Raking his floppy dark hair straight back, he managed a half-smile at Sunni. "Cool."

"Will he pass, Sunni?" asked Munro, from the shadow of his hearse.

"Will he pass as what?" she murmured, staring at her friend.

Munro tickled Lexie under the chin. "As a cowboy buccaneer about to embark on a secret mission maybe?"

"Uh-huh."

"More like Zorro. Thanks, I'll get your things back to you tomorrow." Blaise put his jacket back on and stuffed his shirt half into its pocket. "Let's go."

In the Mariner's Chamber, he took off the black eye mask and laid it on the bench as he watched Munro place a new wick in the oil. Nobody would be bothering them after the spirit photographer had told Jimmy that they were assisting him in getting ready for his Halloween show. And the door was securely locked against the hooded guy.

"You okay?" he whispered. "Ishbel's here, isn't she?"

"Yeah, she's getting ramped up but I don't think she can follow me," Sunni muttered, batting at invisible fingers pulling strands of her wig. "Hurry up, Oculus!"

"Ready?" Munro asked, holding up Corvo's slide marked III. "I'm putting this slide in now."

When the chamber went dark and the shadow lantern beamed its transformative light, Blaise felt every muscle melt away, floating somewhere in the ether until he was ready to be rebuilt inside the projection.

He and Sunni materialised in a tiny room with a narrow bed against one wall, lit only by a candle on a small table. He could barely stand under the low-beamed ceiling so he opened a small door, outside of the Oculus's light, and scanned the surroundings. With a finger held to his lips, he stepped out with the candle in one hand.

They crept down a narrow wooden staircase by the light of lanterns dotted about the stairwell and peeped into rooms on the two floors below. On the ground floor was a long corridor with doors at either end. After trying the further one and finding it locked, they opened the other.

Down a few steps, in a low-ceilinged room, Fausto Corvo's figure stood like a sentry next to an arched door. As in the previous two shadowlands, he was still and unseeing. Sunni hovered at the door, partly hidden, and Blaise softly called out, "Greetings, Signor Corvo."

The figure bent into a deep bow. "Welcome to this shadowland, Your Imperial Majesty. It makes my heart joyful that you are here. It means Your Majesty safely received the gift of Fausto Corvo's Oculus and his glass paintings. *Il* Corvo wishes he could greet you himself but he had to flee and hide from the villain Soranzo who covets his secrets. I am *il* Corvo's double, painted and brought to life by his own hand and the power of the heavens. For your Majesty's pleasure and knowledge, I will act out the next chapter in *il* Corvo's story. If you look carefully you will also find clues in the hunt for the three enchanted paintings he made for you. In a moment you will learn how *il* Corvo hid in Amsterdam in the spring of 1583 after he escaped from Prague. Do not be afraid of what you see in this shadowland, Your Majesty. Follow me, then come back to this place and you will return home safely."

When he had straightened up, the double opened the door and swept one arm towards the dark world outside.

"Come on." Blaise hurried down the stairs and strode towards the door. But as he tried to pass through it, Corvo's double grabbed his jacket sleeve.

"You are not His Majesty," he said, his black eyes flicking in the way Blaise now recognised. "You shall not pass."

"But we are friends of Fausto Corvo and we're here to help protect the three lost paintings."

"That is not possible. Turn back and leave this place," ordered the double.

Blaise hurried back to the stairs and made great show of leaving with Sunni. After a moment's wait he peeped out as the double walked out of the door himself. "Come on."

He put the candlestick down on the lowest stair and they bounded to the door. Outside was a black canal, shining under a full moon. No road or pavement, just water lapping against the foundation of the house and its tiny dock just above the water level. There was not one light in the tall row of buildings opposite, with their gabled roofs and arched windows.

"Oh no," Blaise muttered, catching sight of Corvo's moonlit double gliding away in a small rowing boat.

"There's another boat," whispered Sunni. "Let's take it."

"Okay," he agreed. "You got something bright we can leave behind as a marker? These houses all look the same in the dark."

Sunni clutched Rhona's white cardigan around her but after a moment she reluctantly hung her white wig on a wooden post by the dock. "Can't miss that."

"Great." After a struggle to keep his balance, Blaise boarded the second rowing boat and extended his hand to Sunni. She dropped awkwardly onto the seat opposite him. "Make sure we don't lose the clone."

Oars in hand, he pushed the craft away from the dock. With each stroke, the water glimmered and sparkled, and he began building up to a decent speed.

"Don't worry." Sunni straightened her white gown, squinting into the gloom. Suddenly her voice came quick and edgy. "Another boat's coming in the opposite direction."

"Who's in it?"

"Can't tell, it's too far away," she hissed. "But the clone stopped rowing. He's watching it."

Blaise looked over his shoulder and pulled hard at the oars.

"Almost," she said under her breath. "Just a bit further." A moment later she whispered, "Now! Ease up."

Blaise glanced round and moved their boat in close to the double's. He kept the oars poised and let them drift round so he could see what was happening.

"You were told to go!" said Corvo's double, grim-faced. "Return the craft and leave this shadowland."

"Sorry," said Blaise. "We need to stay."

The third boat approached, slow and muffled. Lapping water and the bump of wood on wood grew louder until he could make out a solitary figure rowing.

When it was close by, Blaise peered at the rower.

The moon played on the man's wide hat but his face was in darkness. As the third boat drew parallel to their boat, the stranger raised his chin.

Sunni let out a cry of fear. When Blaise saw the rower's heavy-lidded eyes and flattened nose, livid white in the moonlight, he tried desperately to keep his composure.

"He's just a clone," Blaise said. "He can't be real."

The rower raised one arm and flung something silvery over the water. A set of keys hit the wooden bench beside Sunni.

"I am no clone." Soranzo's silky voice bounced across the canal and echoed from the houses. "I can hear your whispers and I see past your costumes, Master Blaise and Miss Sunniva."

Chapter 13

Sunni's insides froze.

"We met in London," Soranzo said smoothly. "In both the eighteenth and the twenty-first centuries."

"He *is* real," Blaise breathed. "He knows our names."

Sunni was still quaking inside. Only a couple of months before, this man had made them prisoners in a garret of young forgers, punishing them for keeping Corvo's secrets, until she and Blaise escaped into the desperate streets of eighteenth-century London.

Soranzo's voice hardened. "Our time together was… unsuccessful."

"Because we wouldn't tell you anything," Blaise sputtered. "And we never will."

Corvo's double sat motionless in his boat, his face slack and his eyes darting wildly.

"I shall find what I need by myself," said Soranzo, glancing disdainfully at the double. "That husk of Corvo's is worthless. See how our presence confuses his fragile brain – if he has one."

"He'll only talk to Emperor Rudolf," Blaise said, head held high as he kept their rowing boat steady.

"I already know this, boy," Soranzo sneered. "I know all about these shadowlands."

Sunni's fear gave way to anger. "How did you get in? And how can you still be here?"

"The same way as you arrived, I presume. Through Corvo's glass paintings inside the Oculus." Their adversary frowned and murmured, "In the year 1583."

"How did you *get* the Oculus?" she shouted.

"No more questions," said Soranzo. "Unless perhaps you wish to ask one of this creature." He jutted his chin towards Corvo's double. "Ask him where his satchel of paintings is."

Sunni and Blaise both stared at the clone, whose mouth opened slightly as his eyes worked back and forth. There was no familiar long satchel across his back. As she thought back, Sunni realised it had not been there when they had first seen him at the door.

Without waiting for an answer, Soranzo said, "The satchel is nowhere to be found."

"Don't ask us," said Blaise. "We don't know anything about it."

Soranzo took a deep breath in and out. "I have met a man called Lorimer Bell," he said evenly. "Those are his keys by your side, Sunniva. He would like you to return them to Blackhope Tower. He will not be needing them here."

"*You* have Mr Bell!" yelled Blaise. "Let him go!"

"Do not shout at me," Soranzo hissed. "This Lorimer Bell means something to you. Then I shall release him." He leaned forwards. "After you do something for me."

Sunni picked up Lorimer's keys and held them so tightly, they dug into her flesh. "Why would we ever do anything for you?"

"I had hoped to go to Blackhope Tower myself after we

parted company in London," said Soranzo, ignoring her.

"Parted company! You mean after you burned Jeremiah Starling's house to the ground," Blaise said tersely. "And you left us to die."

"You survived. So did Starling and his young forgers. And I returned to the year 1583." Soranzo's boat drifted away slightly. "I planned to enter *The Mariner's Return to Arcadia* through the labyrinth, which is still open in my century, but I obtained the Oculus instead. And I crossed the shadow lantern's light into that peculiar Venice, then Prague and now this strange Amsterdam."

"And you've been here ever since," said Blaise.

"An unfortunate error." As his boat drifted and turned, the moonlight highlighted a gleam in the man's eyes. "I am surprised so much time has passed. These shadowlands must sleep when the Oculus is not in use."

"But you can leave now, the same way you came in. So why don't you?" Blaise sneered.

"You take me for a simpleton," came the languid reply. "I will not risk becoming a skeleton the moment I step into your century. I know I can never leave this shadowland, but there is perhaps one last place I can go – the place where the actual Fausto Corvo hides with the three enchanted paintings. You will arrange it."

"No," Sunni and Blaise said as one.

Soranzo waved this away. "It is simple. The Oculus is now in the Mariner's Chamber. You will return there and shine this Amsterdam onto *The Mariner's Return to Arcadia*. Then I will send back your Lorimer Bell."

Sunni locked eyes with her friend and saw he was

as surprised by this as she was. "What would happen if Corvo's magic in one place mixes with the other?"

Blaise muttered, "Maybe he thinks it'll form some sort of magical bridge so he can get into *The Mariner's Return* like he wanted."

"You dare to question me again?" Soranzo's figure stiffened and he thrust his oars down into the water. His rowing boat suddenly veered towards theirs, knocking into the startled clone's in his haste. "I know things that your small brains can never comprehend."

"Blaise, go!" Sunni screamed, and he managed to pull their boat around. He rowed furiously towards the house they'd arrived in, with Soranzo at their backs.

"This time you will do as I command!" he bellowed. "Or you will not see Lorimer Bell again."

"Keep going, Blaise!" Sunni couldn't bear to look at the man's face, masklike in the moonlight, so she concentrated on the houses, hunting for the wig on the post. When she spied it in the distance, she whispered, "We're almost there. Pull in hard when I say."

After passing six more houses, she said, "Now!"

His arms quaking, Blaise rowed up and collided with the narrow dock, grabbing hold of one of the wooden posts. "Get out! Hold the rope for me!"

Sunni clambered out and yanked the rope around a post, holding fast while Blaise hoisted himself from the rowing boat.

Soranzo ploughed his boat straight into theirs and let out a long laugh.

Sunni was caught for a moment in his ice-cold gaze.

With a shudder she grabbed her wig, bolted inside and up the stairs, candle in hand, not stopping till she and Blaise were back in the small bedroom, doubled over and gulping for air.

As the projection's light bathed them, she could still hear Soranzo's laughter, but it was far away.

"We're okay," she gasped. "I think he's still outside."

"What if we made a mistake?" Blaise lifted his head. "Maybe we should've stayed and fought him to get Mr B back!"

To Sunni's surprise he went to pull her out of the light and back into the shadowland, but it was too late. His body dematerialised into a web of dancing sparks.

Blaise was still muttering when they were back in the Mariner's Chamber. "We fell for it… he got us to come back."

The overhead light came on in an instant and Munro bustled over to them. "What happened? You were barely gone for five minutes."

Sunni uncurled her hand and Lorimer's keys fell to the floor with a clatter.

"Are you all right?" Munro put a hand to his forehead. "Oh, this wasn't a good idea…"

"Just a tough landing," Blaise mumbled. "But I'm fine." He took a deep breath and got to his feet, slapping dirt off Munro's borrowed shirt. Then he pulled Sunni up and angrily swiped the keys from the floor.

"We were chased out of Amsterdam on purpose."

"Amsterdam this time?" Munro screwed up his face. "Who chased you?"

"You know about Soranzo?" Blaise asked, collapsing into a folding chair.

"Yes," said the spirit photographer, his eyebrows raised. "They say he and his spies chased Corvo all over the world trying to steal his three paintings."

Blaise fiddled with the keys in his lap. "That creep's inside this projection – and he's the real thing, straight from the year 1583."

"But he must have died hundreds of years ago!" Munro exclaimed.

"No, he's still alive in there," said Blaise.

"And looking for the lost paintings..." Munro's eyes were wide.

"Soranzo's holding Mr Bell hostage," said Sunni forlornly, adjusting her white wig over her hair.

"He gave us Mr B's keys as proof," Blaise added.

Munro's face twisted in sudden anger. "Why on earth did Lorimer go in there? He had no right to use my property, especially after giving me a lecture on responsibility."

"I don't know," said Blaise. "But he did and it's screwed everything up."

"Was Corvo's clone there?"

"Yeah, but he was pretty out of it," Blaise said. "And there's another big problem."

"Just one?" Munro snorted.

"Soranzo gave us an ultimatum," he answered. "He said he won't give Mr Bell back unless..."

Sunni hung her head. "Unless we aim Corvo's third slide onto that painting."

"Why would he want to do that? It doesn't make sense."

"We think he wants to get inside the painting and he believes the projection will magically connect them somehow. Maybe nothing would happen… but I don't know." Sunni's face sagged, making her look all the more like a melancholy ghost girl. "But he'll do anything to get those lost paintings."

Munro's jaw dropped. "Are you saying they're hidden inside *The Mariner's Return*?"

"I-I don't know," said Sunni.

"We don't know anything!" Blaise shot her a warning look. "Except that Soranzo's a nutcase and if he thinks we're going to follow his orders, he's dreaming."

A cool breeze circulated around Sunni's shoulders, lifting her wig hair at the ends.

"We're not beaming the Amsterdam slide onto *The Mariner's Return*. No way." He stood up and handed Lorimer's keys to Munro. "But we have to go back in and try to find Mr Bell."

Munro was incredulous. "You're in way over your heads."

"Look, we won't do anything stupid," Blaise said firmly. "We'll just figure out where he is and come back for help."

"I don't like it," said Munro.

"We don't either, but we can't leave Mr Bell in there!"

"All you're doing is searching – nothing else!" said Munro. "Don't tangle with this man Soranzo."

Blaise nodded. "No worries. You ready, Sunni?"

"Yes," said Sunni, though she wasn't sure she was.

She heard jaunty music coming from the Great Hall as the band did their sound check and wished she could go there instead, but there was no way out of this. They couldn't just leave their teacher.

"Can you fire up the Oculus please, Munro?" Blaise put his phone, house keys and sketchbook on the bench. "I'm leaving these here for safekeeping."

As Sunni laid her valuables next to his, invisible hands began yanking and pulling at Rhona's cardigan until Sunni said through gritted teeth, "I knew you'd turn up." Before she could do anything to resist, the cardigan was peeled back over Sunni's shoulders and pulled hard backwards.

"No, not this!" She bent her arms and hunched herself tightly. "I need to get out of here, now!"

"All right. Just a moment," Munro mumbled.

The breeze grew frigid and whipped round the Mariner's Chamber, sending the Oculus's newly lit flame into a wild dance. Munro called out soothing words to Lady Ishbel, trying to protect the magic lantern.

A harsh whisper came past Sunni's ear, babbling words she could not make out. *She cannot hurt me, she cannot hurt me*, Sunni thought and began to hum.

"You'd better catch your cat or she'll end up in the projection with us," said Blaise, eyeing Lexie's form sneaking closer to Sunni.

"Come here, old girl. Wouldn't want to lose my business partner, would I?" Munro scooped Lexie up and hurried towards the light switch. "What if you don't have Lorimer Bell with you when you return?"

"Bring us back no matter what," Sunni said.

"Right," said Munro with a grim smile. "Good luck."

The chamber went dark and the Oculus sparked into life, sending out its dancing beam and projecting the third slide on the wall again. Sunni wondered what would happen if she touched Blaise's hand, and inched hers towards him, but in that moment the transformation began and she was whisked onto her own trajectory, ravelling and unravelling.

"Look at that, my lovely," Munro said to Lexie, as he watched Sunni and Blaise materialise on the wall. "What do you make of it?" The cat squirmed in his arms and gave him a look. "All right, I think the projection is high enough off the ground for you to walk about."

She sniffed around in the dark corners of the Mariner's Chamber and finally hopped onto the bench for a nap.

Munro never took his eyes from the small bedroom projected on the wall, even when Sunni and Blaise left it one at a time. When they had vanished into the shadowlands of Amsterdam, he picked his way over to *The Mariner's Return to Arcadia* and moved the rope barrier away from it.

"Sorry, kids, change of plan. I'm with Soranzo on this one. A magical bridge into Corvo's painting? That's worth a try." He placed his gloved hands on the Oculus's sides and slowly shifted it clockwise until the projection lined up exactly with the painting.

"Perfect," he said, pulling off his warm gauntlets and letting them cool down.

The projection lit up Fausto Corvo's vivid painting in the dark. The dark, candle-lit colours of the Amsterdam bedroom mixed with *The Mariner's Return*'s bright blue sky, castle and busy medieval city.

"Now," said Munro, his eyes bright. "Let's see what happens next."

Chapter 14

Sunni and Blaise tiptoed down the dim staircase in the Amsterdam house. Blaise carried the candlestick high in the air, looking all around in case Soranzo should leap from the shadows.

"You think we can get past Corvo's clone without waking him up?" Sunni whispered.

"It seems like it's voice-activated," answered Blaise. "Let's keep quiet and see what happens."

Corvo's double was in the same position as before, standing still and blank-faced by the door.

They tiptoed past and opened the door to the canal, full moon and tall houses opposite. Sunni closed it as quietly as possible but the double's voice began droning on the other side.

Sunni shook her head. "He's off again."

"Doesn't matter," Blaise said as he fiddled with the boat's rope. "I think we should go our own way this time. It's Soranzo we need to watch out for."

"Where do you think he is?" Sunni studied the crooked houses from top to bottom, shuddering to think that their enemy might be watching them from one of the black windows.

"Who knows?"

"He might even be watching us now." Sunni looked down into the inky water and its jagged silver reflection of the moon.

"He'd better not be." Blaise jumped down into the rowing boat and held out his hand to her.

She'd seen Blaise in everything from his school uniform to jeans to an eighteenth-century masquerade costume, but she'd never seen him look like he did in his borrowed gear. There was something steely about him that made her feel slightly breathless. Sunni couldn't help snatching glances at him, his belt buckle glinting in the moonlight.

"I'll row and you look out for Soranzo this time," she said, setting her wig onto the post and holding up her ghostly gown as he helped her manoeuvre down onto the middle seat. Blaise slid the ropes off and she moved them out into the canal just as Corvo's clone opened the door and climbed down into his own rowing boat.

"The clone just got into his boat," she said.

"Does he look like he's in a hurry?" Blaise glanced over his shoulder. "Like he's after us?"

"Not really."

"I wish we could see what happens to him. Man, why did Mr B have to interfere?"

"The sooner we find him, the sooner we can ask," she said.

As they followed the snaking canal, Blaise kept a keen eye on their surroundings from roofs to waterline.

"Hold on." He pulled himself higher against the boat's hull, alert. "Something's weird."

She slowed her rowing and looked around.

“The houses,” he said. “They’re changing.” He pointed up at the roofs. Some houses seemed to have sunk partway into the water and others had grown higher, uneven like tombstones on a hill. Dark water sloshed against the ones they’d just passed. A couple were sliding down inch by inch and sending ripples back that made the boat totter slightly.

Over the now uneven line of roofs, Sunni noticed a patch of midnight-blue sky had gone pale. A robin’s-egg blue was bleeding into it, bringing wisps of white cloud. It was beautiful, as if someone had opened a window in the sky.

“Blaise, look!”

A light grey mist bloomed in another area, obscuring the stars. And in a distant part of the night sky, the sun rose in a splash of pink and gold, like it was peeping through a celestial porthole. It was as if dawn, day, dusk and night were all happening simultaneously above them.

She felt a pinch of fear. "How can the sun be coming up and going down at once? How can there be a sun at all?"

"Something's wrong." Blaise tensed into a hunch, trying to look everywhere at once.

Like some sort of slow-moving airship, a chunk of brown earth and green vegetation broke through the night sky and hung there above them, motionless. Even from below, Sunni could see hills, trees and boulders sprouting from it. Another appeared where a house had been, and another stuck out from a roof, lit by sun from somewhere else.

Suddenly a new shape emerged one bit at a time, pale grey against the sky. By the time it had fully materialised, blocking out the stars, she had already recognised it.

Sunni ran her hand over her face, smearing off some of her pale make-up. "That looks just like the castle from the top layer of *The Mariner's Return*... Something's pushing it through!"

"No way." Blaise's voice shook with anger. "It's got to be Munro. He must have projected the slide onto the painting when I told him not to!"

"That would explain why the sky's all jumbled up."

"Yeah, the Oculus's projection is penetrating the painting! Everything's merging." Blaise's voice echoed against the towering houses. "I can't believe Munro's stabbed us in the back. We've got to stop him. Turn the boat around."

She stopped rowing. "What, go back?"

"You got a better idea?"

"Yeah!" she said. "Find Mr B. That's the plan."

"It'll be chaos when all the under-paintings in Arcadia merge with this place. We've got to stop Munro, Sunni!"

"Let's find Mr B and get out," she said, trying to keep calm. "Soranzo's got what he wants now, so he'll have to let him go anyway."

"Sunni, this city will be filled with predators any minute. And Soranzo will be able to walk straight into Arcadia. We can't let that happen."

"What are we going to do, tie Munro up so he can't mess with the Oculus?" she scoffed. "Then who's going to watch the flame?"

"I don't know… we'll get James and Iona. Come on, there's no time!"

"Fine." Sunni gripped the oars so tightly her knuckles were white. "I hope you're right." She turned the boat and rowed as if her arms were pistons, past sinking and rising houses, sections of the canal that were black as pitch and others that were lit by shafts of sunlight. She steered around eddies that bubbled up from nowhere, aiming for flat water, and repeated to herself, *row, row, row.*

"Good, Sunni, keep going!" Blaise urged.

But as she made the next curving turn, Blaise gasped at what lay ahead and she glanced over her shoulder. An island was growing up and out of the front walls and windows of the houses before them. Its trees tickled the windows and great red, blue and yellow tropical birds darted out, squawking. The force of the emerging land pushed waves at the rowing boat and propelled them backwards.

"Get around it!" Blaise shouted.

"I'm trying!"

Sunni carefully worked the oars and managed to steer them through the only strait of water available. One oar scraped a wall and Blaise had to push the hull away from the rough bricks as they bumped into houses. The water was so high against some buildings that they could look into the third-floor windows of one sunken house and onto the roof tiles of another.

The boat burst through into clear water and Sunni gulped at the air, though never let up rowing at her fierce pace.

"I can see your wig on the post. We're almost back where we started," Blaise said. "You want me to take over?"

"Leave it!" she retorted, glancing over her shoulder again. Feeble light from a distant sunrise lit up a rectangle of water, warming it to a muddy brown. Sunni could see a disturbance below the surface, causing ripples and small splashes.

"What is that?" she gasped.

"I don't know. Just go around it."

Sunni rowed like a demon, determined to get past. Just as she was about to skim over the area, something black broke the water, rising like a wide shiny hill across the width of the canal and blending in with the houses on both sides.

"Oh, man!" Blaise exclaimed. "Sunni, stop!"

The rowing boat skidded up onto the ebony form and toppled to one side, knocking Blaise from his seat and sending the oars flying. Sunni tumbled out and rolled down into the water. She found something hard and narrow just below the surface and grabbed it with both hands.

Blaise eased himself from the rowing boat, clinging spread-eagled to the wide dark hill, and the craft slid down into the murk, quickly bobbing away.

"Sunni?" he called in a low voice. "You okay?"

"Sort of. I'm just below you now." She clung tight with both hands as her body floated. She shimmied sideways and felt her way along the submerged object until she came to the place where it joined the hilly surface Blaise clung to. He had managed to edge his body upwards and find a more level place to rest.

"Try to get up here," he said. At the sound of splashing behind them, he added urgently, "Find a toehold and climb."

Sunni tried to hoist herself up but fell back. "It's slippery! There's nothing to grab onto." She kicked at the object she clung to, looking for a place for her feet to catch hold so she could hoist herself up. Whatever this thing was, it went down far below the surface. Suddenly it jerked upwards, dragging Sunni with it as it breached the water. A massive spiny fin curled above her, waving and dripping. It was attached to a monstrous sea snake.

"Are you still here, lady spirit?" Munro called into the dark of the Mariner's Chamber. "Why won't you reveal yourself again?" After a silent moment he shrugged and spoke to his dozing cat. "Rest while you can, my love. If I'm right, we are going to be busy tonight. The lady may not wish to show herself to us but others will."

He briefly glanced inside the Oculus and watched the projection play on the surface of the painting. "Plenty of oil and a hearty flame, Lexie. And while the kids are busy in there, we can watch for spirits." Munro crouched down and touched one of the floor tiles that had once made up the labyrinth. "This chamber is potent, Lexie. I can feel it! We're in the centre of a magical world, the *axis mundi* of Fausto Corvo's power. The labyrinth may be gone but the spirits of all the Mariner's Chamber's unknown skeletons are just waiting to make themselves known this All Hallows' Eve!"

He felt about in his waistcoat and large coat pockets and began laying objects on the table, catching the reflected light of the magic lantern: his camera, his pocket watch and a folded-up Ouija board. With trembling hands, Munro carefully spread the board out and took an indicator from his waistcoat. He ran his index finger over the letters, numbers and words printed on the board: *Yes, No, Goodbye.*

"There, my dear, everything is ready," said Munro, turning to watch the projection on the wall. "When the skeletons' spirits come, we will capture them on film."

Lexie's eyes blinked open and fixed on something in the dark.

A figure moved through the woods and onto Blackhope Tower's lawn, where he blended in with a few revellers entering the castle. He waited outside the door until a large and boisterous group arrived, brandishing their tickets, and slipped in with them. The tired-looking guard, one of Jimmy's minions, just waved the party through and they moved upstairs as a unit, giggling and insulting each other without noticing they'd attracted a straggler.

When one of the women at the rear of the group missed a step on the spiral staircase and began falling backwards, the wiry figure caught her and shoved her forwards. She turned to say thank you and her face froze at sight of her rescuer, a ninja dressed in black from head to toe, with only a horizontal slit revealing his eyes.

She gave him another spooked look as they walked from the stairs to the Great Hall and whispered something to a companion. The ninja hesitated and pressed against the stairwell wall until they were gone. After a few moments, he sneaked to the Great Hall's entrance and cast his eyes over the crowded room, looking for two particular faces. Satisfied that they were not at the fancy dress party, he tiptoed up to the next floor, flicking on a torch concealed in his palm.

There was a faint line of amber light showing from under the Mariner's Chamber door, indicating someone was inside. The ninja went close and put his black-clad ear to the wood, listening intently. His body tensed at the sound of a male voice saying something in a wheedling tone on the other side. Gripping the door handle with a gloved hand, he slowly turned it, on alert for any creaks, and pulled.

After three failed attempts, he gave up on the locked door. Hot anger coursed through him, and he punched one palm with the knuckles of the other hand to calm down. Stealing the guard's keys was too risky. There had to be another way in.

The ninja's eyes narrowed to slits when a new idea came to him. It too brought risks and would force him to emerge from the shadows, but it might work. Like a scorpion scuttling from hiding place to hiding place, the ninja headed back to the spiral staircase and went downstairs. He picked up a discarded drinks cup from the floor and sauntered nonchalantly towards the Great Hall as if he belonged there.

Chapter 15

Sunni's high wail echoed against the Amsterdam canal buildings. Blaise's stomach turned upside down at the sound and there was nothing he could do to help her. His sore fingers dug into the sea snake's skin and though his feet were wedged firmly enough for the moment, his arms were tiring. This slimy beast also stank of brine and rotting fish and Blaise's face was mashed right into it.

"Sunni!" he called out, wishing he had eyes in the back of his head.

But her wails had become whimpers and she didn't answer. Blaise didn't see any way out of this one and his eyes stung with sweat and tears.

"Sunni." He could barely get her name out. "I'm sorry I got us into this."

A series of hiccupping yelps came from somewhere behind him. He tried to crawl somewhere, anywhere, but he was splayed out like a starfish drying on a rock. Exhausted, he laid his head down and squeezed his eyes shut, sensing a rippling movement under him, as if muscles were flexing and stretching below the black thing's surface. The ripples came in stronger waves and his body undulated with them, pushed higher and lower.

He managed to look round but saw no sign of her.

What if she was dragged under and trapped? What if she's… drowned?

Suddenly the snake shifted. Clinging on even more tightly, Blaise stared blankly at a white thing that had floated out across the black water. It was Sunni, her legs churning up and down as she propelled herself away.

Blaise let go and rolled off the monster's back. After thrashing through the water, he managed to reach her and grab hold. Sunni jerked at his touch, begging him to leave her alone.

"It's me," he breathed, holding her arm tight.

"Get away from it," Sunni gasped, struggling against him, trying to get further out into the canal.

He glanced back and in the muddy light he saw the giant sea snake with several sets of barbed wings studded in its sides, writhing and undulating. Its thinner tail end had merged with the top of one house, while its head and neck were embedded in the foundations of the house opposite.

"Let's get out of here," Blaise sputtered, "in case that thing gets loose."

"Over there." Sunni pointed at a partly submerged doorway a few houses down from the sea snake. "Get inside that house."

He coughed up some water. "Okay."

They dog-paddled through the inky water and felt their way along the house's rough bricks. Blaise got a toehold on the doorframe and grabbed the handle. He managed to yank it open and crawl inside as canal water flooded over him and into the room. Sunni struggled in after him and together they waded up into the corridor.

Sunni, whose streaked make-up and streaming hair made her look like a drowned zombie, stumbled out into the cobbled street first, panting.

"We're all right," she kept repeating.

"This is messed up," Blaise said, hanging his head. "Sunni, I am really, really sorry. You almost died." Water streamed from his shoes, trousers and Munro's sodden shirt.

"So did you," she gasped. "For only about the hundredth time." She wrung her hair out and shook water droplets from her gown. "Come on. We've got to go!"

"Yeah."

They moved quickly through a street that was half midnight and half sunset, with a sulphurous ochre light that made long shadows everywhere. Arcadia's tree roots pushed up the cobbles and foliage grew from bricks. Flower-lined dirt paths disappeared into the walls and birds warbled from invisible tree branches in the sky. Like the canal, this lane curved round but petered out wherever the woods had appeared.

Blaise thought he recognised these swaying groves as they bushwhacked through. They were from one of the under-paintings below *The Mariner's Return to Arcadia*, near to a sculpture garden, a tangerine-coloured lake and a palace that had been lit by torches of pink light.

He was startled from his memories by a thrashing sound nearby. A man's dim outline staggered from tree to tree, moaning. Without a second thought Blaise advanced towards it, wishing there was more light.

"Careful," Sunni hissed.

The figure doubled over and fell to the ground, shrouded

in a dark cloak like a bat huddled inside its wings.

"Don't go any closer," she whispered. "Could be a trick."

Blaise halted and called out, "Who are you?"

A deep voice rasped a string of words he could not make out.

"I can't understand..." Blaise moved closer.

The man moaned and said more foreign words before gasping, "Your Imperial Highness..."

"Corvo's clone." Blaise was by his side in a flash, rolling him over.

Sunni hunched down. "Is he bleeding?"

"I don't think so," said Blaise. "We are your friends. What happened?"

"I do not understand. This is wrong," the double murmured. "The shadowlands... all wrong."

Something dropped from the double's body and Sunni felt about for it on the ground.

"It's round and metal with a lump in the centre," she said to Blaise. "We saw this in Prague. A pickpocket tried to steal it."

Blaise took it and held the object close to his eyes, tracing the deep indentations around its edge. "Yeah, I remember." He pressed the metal disc into the double's palm and closed his fingers around it.

"What is this thing, sir?" he asked.

"The cipher disc..." Corvo's double breathed and let go of the disc. "For His Majesty..."

"Cipher disc?"

"To find his treasures..." The double began babbling in other tongues, his body jolting and shivering. The only word Blaise could make out sounded like 'rabanus', but he wasn't sure.

"He's losing it. I don't think this was in the script," said Blaise miserably, stuffing the metallic object into his own trouser pocket. "I don't know what to do."

Sunni grabbed his arm. "Nothing we can do."

At first Blaise resisted, but when he heard the sounds coming from the shadowy trees beyond he leaped after her and hunkered down behind some bracken.

Two caped shadows slid from the gloom and fell upon the semi-conscious double. They shook him, talking at him in hushed tones, but their victim only groaned and fell back, limp. Cautiously, like animals sniffing the air for intruders, the pair got up and took a few unsteady steps towards the bracken. From his burly shape and short legs, Blaise guessed one was Zago and the other might be Magno.

They also teetered around, muttering and holding their heads, and with a final prod at the double's body they lurched back the way they had come.

"Shh," whispered Blaise. "Follow me." They edged away, slowly at first, and then breaking into a run when they plunged back into the midnight darkness of the Amsterdam street.

"So you don't think that was supposed to happen?" Sunni asked, breathing hard.

"No." Blaise fingered the metal disc in his pocket. "The clone was definitely malfunctioning."

"I think Zago and Magno were malfunctioning too. They're part of this video diary and its magic is getting screwed up because of Munro."

The street was studded with highlighted fragments hanging in mid-air, as if someone had torn up photos taken at sunset and glued them onto this night scene. Blaise and Sunni dodged a sandaled stone foot on a fragment of plinth, the rear haunches and tail of a lion and part of a sphinx's face.

"That's too creepy! I recognise that sphinx. Pieces of the sculpture garden in Arcadia are bleeding through," Blaise said, with one eye behind them for Zago and Magno, just in case.

"Same as that giant sea snake," said Sunni ruefully.

"This place could look totally different in five minutes if the worlds keep merging. We need to get up really high and see everything. We'll get a better chance of spotting Soranzo and Mr B."

"Top floor of a house?"

"No, higher. But Amsterdam is as flat as a pancake." He paused. "Wait. If Arcadia's sculptures are bleeding through, maybe its hills are too."

"Maybe," she said, nodding to the right. "Wouldn't they be that way from the sculpture garden?"

"One way to find out."

They hastily felt their way past the stone fragments as the sun slid down behind the rooftops.

Blaise thought of something his father said sometimes. "When I have a problem, my dad says to climb up a hill and look down on it. And it's true. Problems seem smaller when you're up there. And even if there's no hill to climb, I imagine I'm up there looking down and that helps too."

Sunni let out a breath. "Hope your dad's right this time."

The sky was blood red behind the sunken higgledy-piggledy roofs, but lit at the same time by the full moon above. One roof had morphed into a huge misshapen lump and was taking over several of the roofs adjoining it.

"Here," said Blaise, putting his shoulder to a door that had a tree growing sideways from it. He pushed hard against it, meeting a springy, scratchy resistance. Managing to open it wide enough for Sunni to get through, he urged her into a dark entrance.

"It's pitch black in there," she protested. "Great."

"I'll go alone if you want."

"No way."

Blaise pressed through the door and into a space tangled with brambles and thorns. Past caring what this would do to Munro's shirt, he raised his arms overhead and headed for the place he guessed a staircase might be.

Tripping onto crooked steps half-covered with pebbly soil and scrubby grass, he scrambled up, with Sunni just behind, and wound round a path that led upwards onto rough ground and vegetation. A few signs of human life popped up, buried in the shrubbery. A pewter tankard gleamed on the path and a scrap of cloth was caught on a thick vine.

The roof had been shucked away by the tremendous heap of dirt, stones and branches that rose under it. Blaise picked his way to an exposed outcrop at the top and directed Sunni, who sank down onto the rock next to him.

As he took in what lay below the multi-coloured sky, he went quiet. The panorama was stunning but disturbing too. It looked like Corvo's recreation of Amsterdam had been a small, self-contained island in a vast ocean of blackness, a compact replica city made up of interlocking streets and canals in concentric circles – but that was before Munro had merged it with *The Mariner's Return to Arcadia*. Now the sky above it was a light show of rising and setting suns, the full moon, mist patches and stars. The heavenly bodies performed all these functions over a city that had now been invaded by forests, islands and sea monsters. Somewhere, in all of that, Soranzo held Lorimer Bell prisoner. Finding them was a big enough problem, but now, as he gazed downwards, Blaise saw they had another one.

"Oh man," he said, pointing down at lights moving in the gloom. "New arrivals!"

Chapter 16

Lexie sat perfectly still on the bench in the Mariner's Chamber, scanning the dim room as if she were following an invisible flying bug. Her master had turned away from the Oculus and was watching the dark corners with her.

Shadows were always full of activity, but not the kind that most people were happy to abide with. They contained watchers and hunters, sounds and smells, but what Munro loved most were the hidden souls who came from the darkness because they knew he would see them. When he was little, he'd seen them hovering at the bottom of his bed or floating in the curtains at his window. They'd never scared him – they'd just made him sad. If spirits resorted to visiting a small boy, it must be very lonely where they lived. So Munro had talked to them when he should have been asleep and they sometimes seemed to answer in whispers.

When he got older he described them to his father and was slapped down for talking nonsense. There were whispers in his village that Munro had the 'second sight' and these were quickly smothered. But sometimes someone would give him a clue about who his spirits might be. A neighbour might mention the story of the ghostly old lady he saw digging in the garden of a deserted, tumbledown cottage, or of the long-dead farmer who still roamed the nearby fields. And then Munro would have something he could talk to the spirits about, even if they didn't answer.

After Munro grew up, he left home and went to the city. The spirits didn't come to him so readily any more, so he began hunting for them. By chance, he saw one through a stained-glass window and set about making special spectacles and goggles with amethyst-coloured lenses. It was no longer good enough to see the ghosts and talk to them. He needed to record them, collect them and keep them forever. That was when he bought his first camera, then a second and a third. Munro liked expensive equipment, antiques and fine clothes, even if he sometimes had to cheat or steal to get them – and spend a bit of time in jail to make up for it.

One day a strange-faced cat appeared on his front doormat and walked in as if she belonged there. When Munro realised that the cat saw the same spirits he did, and many more that he did not, he bought her a collar and some food and gave her a name, assuming the spirits must have sent her to help with his mission.

In a small black notebook Munro wrote the names of places where there were spirits he wanted to meet and capture on film. Over the years he had ticked off many names on the list, but one remained there, fascinating above all others. *Mariner's Chamber, Blackhope Tower, Braeside.*

And here he was. The managers at Blackhope Tower gave him whatever he wished in return for bringing the Oculus to their festival. But they had no idea why he really wanted access to the Mariner's Chamber – so he might find out the location of Corvo's three lost paintings from its spirits. And now Sunni and Blaise were blazing a trail through the slide projections, doing that dirty work for him, just in case.

Munro glanced at the magic lantern and the projection that lit up the huge painting on the wall. There was no sign of the two teenagers there yet, so he turned away.

"Yes!" he breathed, as something brushed round his feet, like a minnow exploring one's ankles in a tidal pool. "Come forth!"

These spirits were hesitant perhaps, lodged for so long among the chamber's old stones, and unused to being noticed. But Munro knew they were there: the ghosts of spies and bounty hunters who had sought Corvo and his paintings in Arcadia and, over the centuries, had escaped the under-paintings only to die and appear on the labyrinth as skeletons.

"Come forth, gentlemen," he said, because he knew all the skeletons, except the last one, had been men dressed in rotted clothing of the distant past. "You all ventured into Fausto Corvo's painting and paid with your lives. Who were you, and what are your stories? I want to know your names and honour your memories!" He summoned them again in simple Latin and Italian and even in French.

Munro turned back to his Ouija board and waited for the indicator to move, but it didn't, so he closed his eyes and touched it lightly with two fingertips. A current shot up into his arm and he jumped with excitement.

"That's right," he said encouragingly. "Come out on this night of nights when the barriers between our worlds are so thin!"

Very slowly, the indicator began moving under Munro's fingers. He watched it start to bounce around the Ouija board, resting on a string of letters that made no sense. Even the cardboard was electric under his fingers, so he knew there were souls struggling to get out, but they just needed time and patience. He told himself it would be worth the wait when he possessed spirit photos of the Mariner's Chamber's skeletons – and they told him what they knew about the three paintings.

Lexie had scarcely moved from her frozen position on the bench. Her eyes still darted about but alighted on nothing. Something was there but it could not get through.

"My friends," he said in a honeyed tone. "You are so keen to let me know who you are that we have a bit of a blockage here. Might I be allowed to meet you one at a time please?"

Something whooshed around Munro's ears and made the cat emit a small squeak, her head circling round and round to see what was flying about the chamber.

"Ah, very good." He lifted his fingers briefly and laid them back onto the indicator. "Shall we begin again?"

The indicator juddered as if it were being pulled in several directions at once.

"Gentlemen," he gently chided. "You will all have a turn."

The indicator was yanked from Munro's hands and stabbed vertically into the board.

The photographer leaped away and Lexie began making a mewling noise he had never heard before. She was up on all fours, tensed and staring at him with her wide green-gold eyes.

Munro slowly turned round.

At first he nearly collapsed at the sight of the misty thing that glowered at him from the darkness. A curtain of long, lank hair half-covered the phantom's face, but what Munro could see was deeply pitted and scarred. There was no eyebrow above the round eye that stared at him. Its tunic and breeches hung from the bony body and it gripped a short piece of rope in its skeletal hand. The thing hovered, never releasing him from its gaze.

"W-welcome, sir," said Munro.

Without taking his own eyes from the ghost, Munro edged over to the table where the neglected Oculus stood. Scarcely able to believe his luck, he felt about for his camera and began snapping pictures. After he'd taken what he believed to be an excellent collection of the spirit, he prised the indicator out of the Ouija board and laid it flat asking, "What brought you to Blackhope Tower, sir?"

The phantom smiled, its mouth a dark toothless slit.

The indicator pulled itself from the board and spelled out two words. MAGICK PAINTINGS.

Munro shivered with excitement. "And did you find the magic paintings?"

The phantom's horrible smile changed into an even more hideous grimace as the indicator covered two letters. NO. The wraith raised its hands high above its head with the rope stretched taut between them, and let out a silent roar of rage.

No problem. We'll see what the other spirits have to say. Hands trembling with delicious terror, Munro took picture after picture, thinking of customers who would pay good money for prints of this one.

Suddenly the indicator sliced itself across the Ouija

board and broke in half as a second wraith with a sabre materialised beside the first. The two apparitions merged at one shoulder, hazy against the dark chamber.

"Welcome, sir."

Lexie's fur stood on end and she was pressed hard against the back wall of the Mariner's Chamber, but Munro took no notice as he captured the two spirits on camera. This was turning out better than he could have hoped and he was going to take full advantage. This new spirit, with its surly expression, long moustache and patch of beard, must surely be another bounty hunter who had once sneaked into Corvo's painting seeking treasure.

Munro took the camera away from his eye. That was strange. The pair of phantoms seemed a bit larger than before. Curious, he quickly scrolled through his previous pictures, trying to decide whether anything had changed. When he looked up, a third spectre had joined the others.

And this one was big – *very* big.

Under its eerily lit spider's web, the Great Hall rang with the sounds of clapping hands and blazing fiddles as pairs of costumed guests stomped and danced. Portly devils, leggy cats and feathered angels drank down cups of blood-red punch and galloped over the stone tiles, occasionally whooping out loud. The music only just drowned out the roar of conversations at the tables that lined the compact dance floor.

When the ninja strolled in, no one paid him any attention

or made any attempt to speak to him. *Perfect*. He smirked as he calculated the best route to the table on the far side of the hall where the zombie prom queen sat.

The girl's face and arms were painted with purple-grey patches of decomposing flesh but the ninja recognised her as Sunni's friend, the one whose house she'd gone to the night before. If there was one way to get to Sunni and Blaise, it might be through this girl in the ruffled ball gown, tiara and corsage of dead roses.

But as he was about to move towards her, a nearby conversation caught his attention.

"I wasn't the last person to see Mr Bell before he vanished. Blaise was," said the teenage girl with copper hair and a witch's hat. "You know, the American guy. Quite cute, always has his head in his sketchbook? And his little sidekick Sunni."

"The two that supposedly transported themselves into the painting upstairs?" snorted a girl with sparkly wings and antennae.

"No 'supposedly' about it," said the witch. "I'm sure they did and so is James."

The other girl raised her eyebrows. "Little bit strange that they, of all people, were the last ones to see Mr Bell, don't you think?" She looked around. "Are they here?"

"They were before," said the witch. "But they've disappeared too."

An older woman in a 1920s dress swooped down upon them. "Not up for the dancing, girls?"

"Hi, Mrs Gordon. We were just talking about Mr Bell," said the witch. "Blaise and Sunni were the last to see him."

She paused and let this idea settle. "In the Mariner's Chamber."

"I know, Iona," Mrs Gordon said, glancing solemnly at the blue-haired woman beside her. "Aurora told me."

"I don't like that room!" Aurora said. "Fausto Corvo's painting always sends shivers down my spine. An old friend vanished there."

Mrs Gordon frowned. "You don't mean Lorimer's cousin Angus, do you? He was a nasty piece of work. Good riddance."

Aurora's cheeks went pink. "That's not like the Angus I knew in school. He was funny and friendly."

"Well, he grew up to become a convicted forger. Then he beat up a guard in this castle and put him into hospital before he disappeared," Mrs Gordon said acidly.

Aurora shrank. "Maybe he was defending himself."

"After breaking in? I think not," said Mrs Gordon. "He was a bad lot and you're deluded if you think otherwise."

"Oh." Aurora hung her head and Mrs Gordon let out a silent breath of triumph.

Iona smiled sweetly and asked, "Have you seen Blaise and Sunni since we came in?"

"They were downstairs earlier on, with the so-called spirit photographer and his cat," said Mrs Gordon with pursed lips. "Personally, I don't believe an animal should be allowed in Blackhope Tower, in case it piddles, but that man seems to get away with it."

"His name is Munro," Aurora murmured. "The cat is called Lexie. They see things that we can't and he photographs them."

"Well," said Mrs Gordon, taking her by the arm and leading her away. "He's nowhere to be seen either. There are far too many people disappearing here. Mind yourselves, girls!"

When the ninja had heard enough, he set off towards Mandy, slipping between tables and overexcited dancers until he came round to the rear of her chair, and stood for a moment, thinking what to say. She was with two adults dressed as Mr and Mrs Frankenstein. *Parents*, he said to himself. *Play it cool.*

She must have sensed he was hovering behind her because she turned round and peered at him as if she were trying to figure out who he was. "Hi."

He cleared his throat. "Hi."

"Do I know you?" she asked.

"Maybe," he said. "Dance?"

She wiggled coyly and answered, "Maybe."

He gestured awkwardly towards the dance floor, annoyed he had to do this, and she trotted off before him, grinning at her parents.

As they pushed into the centre of the Great Hall, where couples were waiting for the next number, she squinted at his eyes again. "Aren't you going to tell me who you are?"

He cocked his head and said nothing. As the band cranked up, Mandy laid one lace-gloved hand on his shoulder and he put his arm around her waist, desperately trying to copy what the other couples were doing.

"Okay, be mysterious then," she giggled. "But do you know how to do this one?"

The ninja barely knew how to do any of these ridiculous

dances so he just grunted. He'd go along with this for a few minutes but he had to get her out of the Great Hall as soon as possible.

The band kicked off and the next thing he knew they were hopping forwards and back, jumping to the sides and clapping. He was at least one beat behind everyone else and his irritation grew.

When he and Mandy were facing one another again, clumsily whirling about and kicking their feet, he asked in a low voice, "Can we get out of here for a minute?"

"What?" Mandy asked, her prom dress flying up as she flicked her feet out. "Why?"

"I want to ask you something."

She screwed up her red lips in a pout. "Ask me here!"

"No, it needs to be somewhere quiet," he said hoarsely, letting go of her and hopping out to the side. "There are too many people about."

"You won't even tell me who you are, so why should I go with you?" She was less flirty when he grabbed her round the waist again and she gave him a wary look.

"I'll tell you who I am if you come with me." He was starting to get riled with all this and knew he mustn't let her hear it in his voice, but it was too late.

Mandy stopped dead and another couple danced straight into them. The ninja pulled her out of the others' path and hissed, "This is very important. You've got to come with me."

"I don't like being ordered about by strangers." She removed his hand from her arm and stared hard into his eyes. "Tell me right now or I'll get my dad!"

“All right, all right,” he said under his breath. “Someone you know is in big trouble. And you’re the only one who can help.”

Chapter 17

From their viewpoint on the Amsterdam hill, Sunni and Blaise saw torches appearing one by one in the distance. Each new flame burst into life and moved in behind others in a procession down one of the darkest streets.

"Who are they?" Sunni hugged herself and rubbed her upper arms, tweezing thorns from her wilted costume with her fingernails. "I can't see anything but torches."

"I don't know. I thought for a minute..."

"What?"

"Nothing," he replied. "I'm probably wrong."

"There are a lot of them, whoever they are," she said. "And they know where they're going."

"Someone's leading them. See, one torch is ahead of the others."

"We'd better investigate," Sunni said.

"I still don't get why Munro went against us," Blaise said angrily. "What's the point? Just to see what happens?"

"I've got a funny feeling about it," said Sunni, frowning. "He knows Soranzo's in here hunting for the paintings. What if Munro wants them too?

Blaise scratched his head. "And he's just helping us so he can get information out of us and find them himself?"

"Could be."

"Well, forget that! He's never finding out anything else from me."

"Me neither."

He lifted his chin. "What's that sound?"

The air was punctuated by a gut-wrenching cry from somewhere below them.

A man's anguished voice bayed the same words over and over, sending a chill through them.

"Who's that?" Sunni whispered.

However much he peered down at the jumbled streets, woods and canals, Blaise could not work out where the cries came from.

"Corrrrrrvo!" The howls came closer. "Fausto Corrrrrrvo!"

"Look there." Blaise pointed at a patch of brightness in a street below. A ragged, bearded man ran disjointedly, only stopping to shout and fling his arms at the sky.

"Corrrrrrrrvo!" As the man reeled round a corner the sound muffled.

"That voice..." Sunni shuddered.

"Who *is* that?" asked Blaise. "He's kind of following the people with torches."

"I reckon we should too," said Sunni. "Come on."

They picked their way off the rocky outcrop and down the scrubby hillside. When they had squeezed through the brambles and onto the street, they followed the bearded man's faint voice into a dim part of the city that had no sunlight streaking in from some other sky. Its formerly flat streets now curved up and down, pushed and pulled out of shape by the mountainous land and dangerous ocean from Arcadia's under-paintings.

When they reached a crossroads, Sunni peered round the corner and put up one hand in warning.

A torch glowed from the high, canopied poop deck of an Arcadian galley ship half-buried in the cobblestones, its oars horizontal as if in motion but unable to move because their ends were melted into walls on either side of the street. The vessel looked like a giant, dead insect pinned onto a board with its wings outspread.

"Seems empty," she whispered.

"Yeah," said Blaise, creeping round the corner. "I knew those torches reminded me of something – I saw sailors with them when I was on one of these boats."

"I never thought I'd ever see a galley again." She screwed up her face. "And now this has bled through from Arcadia."

They moved alongside the empty boat, ducking below the canopy of oars. Pausing below the mighty carved bow and its figurehead of an old man with flowing hair and beard, Sunni said, "Let's go after the sailors."

"Are they going to get us any closer to Mr B?" said Blaise.

"I don't know. Maybe we should split up and search."

"Do you really want to do that?" he asked. Losing her in this maze of distorted streets and canals was the last thing he wanted.

"No."

"We stick together," he said with feeling. "At all costs."

She grinned wanly and scanned the darkness.

"I think they turned that way," said Blaise. "They definitely seemed to be heading towards a bridge."

They hurried off in the direction he indicated. The once silent streets were now alive with the sounds of foliage rustling and birdsong. Even the old houses creaked and groaned as more branches pushed in through their walls and lumps of earth grew up through the foundations. Blaise could even hear splashes from the canals. Were they made by masonry falling into the water or by things that were alive?

One new sound made him stop short and hold Sunni back. High-pitched squeals and guttural snorts filled the air as two large pigs ran from a narrow lane and dashed along their street, pursued by a winged creature. Blaise could not make out what the creature was, but it was setting itself to land, claws out, on the slower pig.

The flying thing circled low and swooped, scattering the pigs, which separated and shrieked off in different directions. The predator forced the second one against a wall. It huddled against the bricks for a moment then scampered off, but it was doomed. The winged creature latched onto the pig's back and carried it away into the night. As they crossed the full moon, Blaise saw its form go limp.

The other pig let loose an agonising cry and went round in circles looking for its companion. Blaise and Sunni stood still and called soothing words to it until it slowed to a stop, whimpering.

"Where did they come from?" Sunni asked.

"You got me." Blaise crouched down on his haunches and put his hand out to the animal, which came a bit closer. "We can't leave this guy alone."

Sunni slowly walked away. "Come on, girl. Or boy. Whatever you are, piggy, follow me."

Blaise cajoled the animal and walked slightly behind it so it would follow Sunni. It followed hesitantly at first then joined them.

"Ignore it, so it doesn't think we're after it." He steered them towards a bridge over a canal. "It looks clear ahead."

When they were halfway across, having constantly checked the black water for any moving shapes, Blaise said, "Stinks here. It's like low tide."

"Low tide times ten." She held her nose between her thumb and forefinger.

"I keep kicking this squidgy stuff with my foot," said Blaise.

"Oh!" She jumped back at the sight of a huge dismembered tentacle, curled up and shrivelling on the stones. The bridge was strewn with chunks of dead aquatic flesh.

"Someone's been here and battled some kind of octopus," Blaise exclaimed. "Let's get out of here!"

They hurried over the bridge and made for a thicket of trees growing across the entrance to the next street. Something had hacked through the branches and brush, leaving a man-sized gap. As Sunni pushed through, a shrill noise came from the bridge.

The pig was going crazy at something, but it wasn't until another octopus tentacle had lifted itself up high, that Blaise could make out its black shape against the unnaturally bright night sky. It slid back into the canal as silently as it had come out, but with the shrieking pig in its grip. And then there was silence.

"Oh, no!" Sunni cried out in horror.

"We can't stop now. Go on!"

They struggled into the overgrown street, following the trail of bent foliage and decapitated branches. When they came to a somewhat more open section of street, Blaise could see a suspicious glow beyond the next bend. At last they came upon one house, seemingly intact, that blazed with light on the three lowest of its five floors. One window on the fourth floor was lit and the top floor was in darkness. But the most intriguing thing was the object hanging from a pole outside the main door: the letters *HV* wrought in iron.

Sunni edged close to a ground-floor window. "It's a workshop, full of tools and things. Hey, that looks like the Oculus!"

Blaise peeked in and saw the half-finished metal object on a workbench. "Looks exactly like it."

"Didn't Munro say the name of the guy who made it for Corvo?" Sunni whispered.

"Yeah. I don't remember it but those initials ring a bell," he said, wrinkling his forehead. "Was it Harry? No, Henry…"

"Henryk!" said Sunni.

"Yeah, that's it. And his workshop's full of sailors. We have to get past them and see what's inside."

"There are too many of them down here. But maybe there's another way." Sunni scurried to the opposite side of the street and gestured to him. "Look. The two houses next door have had their top floors busted open. Their roofs are gone."

He knew where she was going with this. "Maybe there's a way we can climb through from up there."

They sneaked in next door and found the house was a shell, empty of any furniture or decoration. Getting up the first four floors was no problem, but as they climbed up to the fifth-floor landing, they found living bushes instead of a door.

"A hedge." Blaise ran his hands over the prickly twigs. "It's pretty even, like it's been trimmed." He moved alongside it. "And there's an opening."

As he stepped through the gap, Sunni followed. "It could be a maze," he said.

"You mean *the* maze from Arcadia," she replied grimly. "The one with invisible predators in it."

"You don't need to remind me," he said.

"I'll go first," said Sunni. "You'd better keep your eyes peeled for anything behind us." She took the first right turn, guiding them through junctions and turns until the maze walls gave way to bricks and mortar again.

"That wasn't the whole of the maze we went through before," Blaise whispered. "It's like it's been pulled apart."

Sunni sighed. "Corvo's magic is getting pulled apart." From the dim top-floor landing of Henryk's house, they tiptoed downstairs to the room where light shone from behind a half-opened door.

Through the crack, Blaise was surprised to see that the room was a makeshift artist's workshop with a rickety easel in the corner and some sketches of trees and Dutch houses pinned to the wall. He heard the clank of cutlery against china and a man inside grunting as he gobbled food down.

Sunni put her finger to her lips and edged in against

the door. Blaise moved in next to her, desperate to see around the corner.

After more slurping and smacking sounds, a man's voice asked, "Can you not eat in a more gentlemanly manner? You are like an animal at the trough."

This voice, with its slight accent, filled Blaise with loathing. Before today he had believed they would never cross paths with Soranzo again, but here they were with only a slab of wall between them.

Soranzo's companion laughed and continued chewing lustily. When he finally spoke, Blaise nearly collapsed with shock. He grabbed Sunni by the hand and squeezed tight to stop her from making a sound.

"My friend," said Angus Bellini in a hoarse voice. "I've been trapped on an island where the niceties of life didn't matter."

"And I awoke to find myself trapped in this Amsterdam after more than four hundred years," Soranzo retorted. "Four hundred years in a dark dream, waiting for the light to return!"

"At least you woke up to a meal fit for a king," said Angus.

"Fit for an emperor!" Soranzo said. "You say you are called Angus Bellini."

"Yes." Angus slurped something. "And you're Soranzo. I suppose I should be surprised to meet you, but after everything that's happened to me, I'm not."

"You look very much like a former associate in Venice, also a Bellini."

Angus growled, "Let me guess… Maffeo Bellini, the painter you used to get information out of Marin, that snotty-nosed apprentice of Corvo's? I'm not Maffeo – and I'm no reincarnation of him either."

"Of course not. But perhaps you are his descendant. We can help each other in the way Maffeo and I did," said Soranzo with a smile in his voice. "You have just come out of Corvo's painting. You know things."

"Mmm." Angus chewed something else. "Now since Corvo is not answering me no matter how loud I shout his name, you can tell me where I am, how I got here and how to get out."

Blaise could hear the interest in Soranzo's voice. "How could Corvo answer you?"

"Because he controls everything. He banished me onto an island and now he's taken me off it, right? How else did I end up in this place?"

"He did not bring you here." Soranzo paced impatiently across the floor. "You are in a shadowland that Fausto Corvo painted onto a piece of glass. With a flame behind it and a certain special lens, a part of this place can be shown on a wall."

"We call that a projection in my world," said Angus.

"At my command this *projection* is being shown on top of *The Mariner's Return to Arcadia* and it is digging into Corvo's secret under-paintings, mixing them together and merging them with this shadowland of Amsterdam."

Blaise could hear the satisfaction in Soranzo's voice. Sunni shook her head grimly and squeezed his hand.

"You mean this projection pulled me off the island where Corvo dumped me?" said Angus.

"Yes, in a way."

"And how do I get out of here?"

"I will show you how to leave—" Soranzo began.

"Hallelujah." Angus interrupted with an abrupt handclap.

"But you must do something for me first."

At this, Blaise exchanged a withering look with Sunni.

"Go on," said Angus.

"You must first show me where Corvo hides," said Soranzo. "The actual Fausto Corvo, not some shell he animated."

"Hmm." A chair was shoved backwards. "I take it you think this projection will expose his hideaway."

"I hope it will," Soranzo said. "We shall find it together."

Blaise squirmed and Sunni tugged on his hand.

"Because I know what his hiding place looks like and you don't," Angus said.

"Yes." Blaise heard the iciness in Soranzo's reply. "And I know how to leave this shadowland and you do not."

"True."

"I will show you something." Footsteps crossed the room and there was the sound of furniture moving. "Do you know this man?"

"Lorimer!" Angus's chair scuffed the floor again. "He's my cousin. What's he doing here? Why have you got him tied up?"

Muffled cries could be heard in the background as Soranzo said, "He will not reveal his reasons for coming to this place. And little do I care."

"Then give him to me as part of our deal," said Angus. "Without the gag and restraints."

"Very well, but if his young friends do not follow

my orders, he may stay trapped here anyway," said Soranzo evenly. "And you will be as well."

"What young friends?"

"Miss Sunniva and Master Blaise, who are in the Mariner's Chamber at this moment, making certain the projection shines onto *The Mariner's Return to Arcadia*."

Angus exploded. "Those two kids are in charge? And you trust them?"

"They have no choice since their teacher is my prisoner," Soranzo said. "That is correct, is it not, Lorimer Bell? Ah yes, he is nodding."

Blaise squirmed and Sunni tugged on his hand.

"If I know those kids, they'll be up to something," Angus said sourly. A chair scraped and more footsteps thundered across the room.

"What can they do?" asked Soranzo. "If they stop the projection, Lorimer Bell will be trapped here. If they come after Lorimer Bell, I will crush them."

"With my help," fumed Angus. "Those kids and I have unfinished business." He muttered under his breath and said, "There you go, Lor, you can open your mouth now."

"I hope to heaven that Sunni and Blaise stay in the Mariner's Chamber," Lorimer cried out. "And you keep your word to let us go, Soranzo."

"I always keep my word," Soranzo said contemptuously. "Then it is settled. You show me the way to Fausto Corvo and I show you the way back into your century." Soranzo's footsteps echoed as he crossed the room again. "And one more thing. I will not tolerate betrayal, Bellini. Do not think of attempting escape with Lorimer Bell."

Angus scoffed, "Don't worry. I'm not sticking my neck out for him."

"What?" Lorimer was incredulous.

"You feel no sympathy for your blood cousin, Bellini?" asked Soranzo.

"No," said Angus. "What are you even doing here anyway? Answer me that, Lor."

Chapter 18

In the Mariner's Chamber, the three spirits transfixed Munro as they became four, then five, then six growing, hollow-eyed figures, each holding his weapon of choice. They faded in and out, pulsating in the dark, but became clearer with each minute that went by.

Munro put his camera down and watched them. He had more than enough photos but his dream of getting information from these spirits was trickling away. Without the Ouija board he was lost. He could not think of a way to question them out loud without enraging them. If they were all bounty hunters and spies who had gone in to find Corvo's magical paintings, as he suspected they were, they had all died on the labyrinth because they had failed.

What should he do? Ask them their names with no chance of hearing them? Compliment them on something? He couldn't think of anything.

To his surprise a seventh ghost appeared, much like the others and just as intent on staring at Munro.

The spirit photographer shifted uneasily and took a few half-hearted shots of this new addition. He told himself to buck up and interact. He'd never get another chance.

"Gentlemen, there are seven of you here," he said boldly. "You each have one thing in common. You were all inside

Fausto Corvo's painted world. Did you cross paths with each other at all?"

At the suggestion that there were *others* present, the spirits' mouths opened in silent war cries, triggering an ancient thirst to dominate. The first phantom to explode with rage swung his sword round, his broken teeth gritted. The rest followed immediately, blindly fighting each other and whipping up a windstorm that howled round the painted ceiling beams. The Mariner's Chamber was clogged with the seven gigantic spirits, parrying and thrusting, trying to destroy their competitors.

"Gentlemen!" Munro called against the rushing wind. "Please stop this! It is time for you to go back where you came from! Please return to the other side NOW!"

Ignored and drowned out, Munro could only stand and gape as the wraiths morphed and shape-shifted, shrank and expanded, passing around him and even through him. He shuddered as the first spirit flew through his chest and he was filled with the dead man's bloodlust and greed. The others passed through too, whispering of their hatred and envy in Italian and French and languages he could not recognise.

Munro's camera fell out of his hand and clattered to the floor in pieces. He dropped to his knees to retrieve the precious object. That was when he saw Lexie huddled under the bench, the white X as bright as a target across her terrified face.

"I'm sorry, my love," he whispered. "I don't know what to do."

Lexie would not move her eyes from the Oculus's

projection on Fausto Corvo's painting. Munro crawled round to face it, shielding his head from the battling spectres, and stared at it in disbelief. The image on the wall was shifting between light and dark, throbbing with colours and shapes that emerged and then receded. It was neither the Oculus's projection nor Corvo's painting. It was writhing and evolving into a new thing.

At that moment, the flame in the magic lantern shuddered and flickered.

The chamber went a shade darker and Munro uttered a horrified, "No!"

"Let us waste no more time," Soranzo said. "We must find Corvo."

Fired with adrenaline, Sunni nudged Blaise away from the workshop door and began scampering up the stairs. At that moment, everything went dim, even the candles behind them in Soranzo's room.

"This cannot happen again!" she heard Soranzo shout. "What are those idiot children doing? They must keep the Oculus's flame strong!"

Angus mumbled something and there was the sound of furniture being flung aside but Sunni paid no attention. All her attention was focused on getting up the stairs quietly, but it was not to be. Near the top landing she tripped on the hem of her costume and went down hard on one shin.

All went quiet in the room behind them. She crawled up the last few steps and got to her feet. In the dim light Blaise took her arm and guided them back into the hedge maze.

Someone left Soranzo's room and took a few tentative steps up the stairs. Sunni prayed he would not follow and hissed in Blaise's ear, "Faster!"

Then came the clatter of leather on wood as heavy feet ran up the stairs and came after them. The footsteps slowed as their pursuers entered the maze, feeling through the hedges the same way they had.

Blaise pulled Sunni round another turn and collided with a plaster wall that had no opening. They hunched there like two petrified animals, shaking and breathless.

The change in the darkness was imperceptible at first, but gradually Sunni could make out the open roof and the stars in the sky above. Their pale light showed a half-broken wall belonging to the house next door.

"Was Ishbel trying to mess with the Oculus again?" Sunni whispered.

"Maybe," he whispered back. "But Munro must have fixed its flame before it went out completely."

Men's voices rumbled up behind them and a torch now glowed through chinks in the dense hedges.

"Quick!" Sunni jumped to her feet and climbed over the crumbling wall. They crouched down to listen.

"What is it?" Angus's voice sounded further away.

"Nothing," said Soranzo, alarmingly near. "A dead end."

"You saw someone."

"I saw a white shape at the top of the stairs."

"Doesn't sound like one of Corvo's monsters. Let's keep going." Angus was unimpressed. "Hurry up, Lor. And by the way, Soranzo, I want to know what happened to my pigs."

"I know nothing about any pigs!"

When their voices had faded away, Blaise said, "They might hang around outside hoping to catch us when we come out."

"I know."

"So let's go back through Henryk's house and look around the room they were in."

Sunni shook her head. "Why?"

"I just want to see something. Two minutes and then we'll see if they've gone."

"Only if the coast is clear," she replied, not convinced, but she let him lead her out of the maze and down the stairs.

The shabby workshop was empty, except for a mess of bones and fruit pits littering the table, and lit by a single lamp. Blaise stealthily looked out of the window. "They're moving away and the sailors are leaving too. Soranzo's at the front and Angus is with him. He's so hairy he looks like a yeti. And Mr B is limping behind them."

Cords still dangled from a chair in a corner. A balled-up cloth gag lay discarded on the floor. Otherwise there was hardly anything in the room except a few sketching and painting materials on a crooked shelf, the easel and a table with some simple chairs.

"What did you want to look at?" Sunni asked, noticing pieces of sharpened red, ochre and brown chalk on the shelf.

"These."

Blaise went to a sheaf of sketches pinned up on a nail by the rickety easel. He took them down and brought them into the lamplight.

She shrugged. "Why?"

"Because I've seen them before," he said. "I picked them up off the floor of the workshop in the Venice shadowland and the clone burned them. And when we were in the tavern in Prague, some guy had this one." Blaise pointed at a sketch of a landscape with some cows.

"Huh?" Sunni examined it with him. "Henryk wasn't an artist, was he? He built the Oculus and metal things like that."

"These sketches are signed by someone called Bertram Rabanus." Blaise paused and slowly repeated, "Rabanus. I wonder…"

Sunni turned over another sketch and pointed at some handwritten words. "Hey, look."

VYLNLUG LUVUHOM GUULN

"Oh boy," Blaise murmured. He flipped over the others and found two with the words:

VYLNLUG LUVUHOM UJLCF

VYLNLUG LUVUHOM GYC

"The same nonsense as in Venice and Prague," she said. "Why do they keep showing up?"

"More clues for the Emperor?" Blaise pinned the sketches back on the wall and shook his head. "Stupid to waste time on this with everything else going on."

"No, it's not." She sighed. "But we have to concentrate on getting Mr B away from Soranzo."

"We'll get him back," said Blaise. "I know we will. Come on!"

But a small voice inside Sunni was sceptical.

At his suggestion, they went back up into the maze and

left through the house next door, just in case any guards were left downstairs in Henryk's house. Cautiously, they entered the street and set off.

A raven appeared above them, making a soft noise to catch their attention.

"Look," Sunni said and called up to it. "Have you come from Arcadia too?"

"Bound to be. There were loads there," Blaise said, watching the bird. "I bet it's pretty confused."

"I'll set it straight," she said harshly. "Raven, Soranzo's on your master's doorstep. He hijacked the Oculus and he's after Corvo and his three magical paintings. Angus Bellini got off the island your master banished him to and now he's helping Soranzo. And if we don't get our teacher back and stop the Oculus soon, Corvo's magic will be so messed up, we may never be able to leave here. Blaise and I have already used up most of our nine lives, so this is it!"

To their surprise, the raven made a hard turn into the next street. It doubled back and stared at them, then continued gliding overhead, chattering at them.

"I think it wants us to follow," she said.

"Yeah, it seemed to listen to what you said, Sunni."

She swept her hand towards the bird hovering above.

"But who knows where it'll take us?" she protested. "Maybe nowhere near Mr B!"

"I have a strange feeling about this raven," said Blaise. "Are you here to help us?"

The bird let out a resounding screech.

"Is that supposed to convince me?" Sunni asked. "Ravens screech a lot."

"Hang on. Corvo's ravens in Arcadia were really intelligent and did tasks for him. If this bird knows something, I think we should go with it."

"I can't believe I'm doing this," Mandy grumbled as she climbed the spiral staircase. She kept giving the ninja dirty looks, as if he were worse than something she'd trodden on in the gutter. "If my dad finds out, I'm in deep trouble."

"I'm not out to get you into trouble," he muttered. "I wish you didn't have to get involved at all."

"Me too," she sniffed.

He switched his torch on at the top of the steps. "Better not to tell anyone about this. All right?"

"Is that a threat? From the person who's been spying on my friend?" Mandy stopped, turned on her heel and started back downstairs. "You need me, by the way, not the other way round."

The ninja slapped his hand to his head. "Now you're twisting my words! All I want from you is five minutes to help *your* friend. Then you go back to your party and forget I was even here." When she didn't respond, he threw up his arms in disbelief and sank against the wall.

Mandy glanced over her shoulder, frowning. With a resigned air, she resumed climbing the stairs and walked, high heels clicking on stone, to where he stood, head hanging. Arms folded across her chest, she asked, "Are we doing this or what?"

A few moments passed before he raised his masked face. "Yeah."

Her mouth set in a red line, Mandy followed him, arms still crossed as if she were off to do something unpleasant for someone equally unpleasant.

When they reached the Mariner's Chamber, he handed Mandy the torch, shoved Munro's sign away and got down on his knees to peer under the door. Something had changed inside the room. It was almost dark, except for the most minuscule glow quite far inside, and it sounded as though a gale was blowing.

He brought his fist down on the floor and let out a short, hard grunt of desperation.

"What?" Mandy asked, alert now.

"Thing's have gone bad in there," the ninja said, glaring at her through his eye slit. He got up and wiped his hands on his black front. "We need someone to unlock this door."

"Get the security guys."

"No! We have to take care of this ourselves. And fast."

"I'm no lock-picker," said Mandy.

"You've got special powers," said the ninja. "Can't you get a spirit to help?"

"How do you even know that?" she demanded.

"People in this town gossip a lot. It was all over the place today," he muttered. "All I had to do was listen."

Mandy narrowed her eyes. "Wait till I find out which of them has been blabbing."

"Can you get the door open or not?"

"I don't know. But I can't just turn it on like that!"

she said, handing him the torch. "I have to be calm and positive and inviting."

He clutched his head and stalked away. "On you go. Me and my bad vibes will be waiting over here."

The ninja fidgeted until Mandy called him back.

"This is not ideal," she complained. "But I'll do my best." Standing close to the door, she closed her purple-shadowed eyes and circled her mottled zombie arms before her. She reached out and touched the wood with both hands. "Hellooo. Is the spirit of Nell here? Hello, Nell!"

"No?" She cocked her head slightly as if she were listening hard. "Okay then. Is the spirit of Lady Ishbel here? Calling Lady Ishbel. I and another need your help!"

The ninja moved a few centimetres closer as Mandy's eyebrows went up and down. "I know it's a lot to ask and I don't deserve it, especially after last night at my birthday party. But you are the only one who can help, Lady Ishbel. Please come to me."

Suddenly she let out a surprised yelp and hopped back without letting go of the door. "Oh, I can feel you coming through!"

Ahhhh. The breeze curled around them, ruffling Mandy's teased-out zombie hair, and circulating over the ninja.

"I knew you'd come," she said. "I just knew it! Now what we need help with is this door, Lady Ishbel. It's locked, you see, and we need to get inside because something's wrong. You know that, don't you?"

A babble of whispers rode on the current of air and Mandy's eyes opened wide. "You have a problem too?" She listened to the whispers. "You want to go home but you're trapped here. Where's your home – Arcadia? Oh, inside the painting in this room! Well, if you open the door we can take a look."

The air whooshed into the keyhole, pushing mechanisms and levers to new positions until it clicked.

"I can hear it!" Mandy exclaimed. "Well done!"

Ahhhhh. With a resounding clunk, the handle shifted and the wooden door was yanked open by invisible hands. Mandy nearly fell backwards but the ninja caught her and righted her before leaping into the Mariner's Chamber.

He felt wild energies whipping round the dark chamber but forced his way through. Mandy, all flying ruffles and hair, dived in behind him, open-mouthed, and heaved the door shut, calling out, "Thank you, Lady Ishbel, we'll just keep it closed for now, shall we?"

By the light of his torch, the ninja saw Munro on the floor, staring up through his clockwork glasses, the long leather coat spread open like a triangle. His stovepipe hat had rolled away into the shadows and a camera lay in pieces beside him.

The ninja crouched down and held him by the lapel, his ear close to the photographer's moving mouth.

"Gentlemen," Munro jabbered. "Spirits, please, you must return…"

The ninja released him and moved to the Oculus. The magic lantern's table shook and the low flame trembled, but it grew steadily stronger, enough to beam its painted glass slide onto Corvo's painting. The ninja couldn't take his eyes off what was happening on the wall.

Mandy skittered round Munro, calling, "Lady Ishbel, are you all right? I can barely sense you in here!" After a moment, she nodded and said, “Now I get you loud and clear. I know it’s Halloween but I feel that there are loads of other spirits in here too!” She wrinkled her forehead as she listened. “You want to know what’s wrong with the painting? Just a minute.”

She grabbed the ninja’s shoulder and shook it.

“Okay, mister, we got you in and now I want answers,” Mandy hissed into his ear. “What’s going on here?”

“You should just go. Better if you stay out of this.” He answered without moving his head. “Thanks for getting me in.”

“You’re having a laugh,” she said, her anger making her zombie complexion even more violet. “You expect me to just slouch off after seeing this? And you owe Lady Ishbel after she helped us!”

“I’ll handle it,” he said through gritted teeth.

“You’ll handle *this*? I’ve never felt as many bad spirits in one place!” She turned full circle, sweeping her arms round the chamber. “You’ve got no clue.”

Before he could open his mouth, something black darted out from under the bench and leaped into Mandy’s arms, clinging on for dear life.

“Ouch!” Wincing, she peeled one of Lexie’s paws off her shoulder and the other off her arm, leaving red punctures and scratches. “That hurts.” She cradled the cat and her face softened. “I’m not leaving. Now tell me where Sunni is before I throttle you.”

“I think she’s in there.” The ninja pointed towards the projection on *The Mariner’s Return to Arcadia*. “And I have no idea how to get her out.”

With a grunt of exasperation he grabbed his mask and yanked it off.

Chapter 19

The raven led Sunni and Blaise across tumbledown lanes, newly emerged fields, islands floating a few feet up in the air and sun-drenched sandbars that had washed in over cobblestones.

"I'm so busy trying not to fall over, I can't tell where we are," said Sunni.

Blaise panted, "I know what your next question is. How far are we from the bedroom we arrived in? Not sure, but it's definitely the other side of town. And will we know how to get there? We'd just better!"

"If we can body-swerve sea snakes, octopus tentacles and pig-snatching birds," said Sunni, hoisting up her now ripped gown as she clambered over another obstacle.

"They were probably Angus's pigs," he said, wincing. "Remember Corvo gave him some for his desert island?"

"Yeah."

The raven chattered to itself, swooping and circling, as it guided them to the city's edge. An opening in the row of houses led to a long quay where many wooden ships were moored. The sea rolled in black waves under the night sky streaked with the distinctive robin's-egg blue that Blaise recognised from *The Mariner's Return to Arcadia*. The moored vessels were strange and brightly lit hybrids –

part ship, part house, part forest – dotted with people from the same painting.

And the ships were moving. One by one an invisible hand cut them loose from their ropes and the kaleidoscopic vessels began shifting out towards a patch of mist hovering over the sea, not very far out.

The raven fixed its gaze on Sunni and Blaise. With tremendous flapping and a guttural clacking sound, it forbade them to go anywhere but to the right and onto a ship whose mooring was still intact.

"It wants us to drift out into the sea like the others," Sunni said, horrified. "No way."

"I know," Blaise muttered, starting to question his own judgement. This raven might be confused after all, tainted by the mixed-up magic in this world. "There is something in the mist, though. The ships are clustering around it but I can't make out what it is."

"Ugh," Sunni said. "It's that fog from Arcadia. You could hide an elephant in it."

Blaise watched the mist grow and diminish, pulsing in and out around something tall and dark. One by one the ships floated to it and stopped. As they slid in together, they created a crazy patchwork of medieval houses and pieces of winding streets – an ethereal floating village.

"You're right," said Blaise, astounded by the beauty of this strange flotilla surrounded by smoky mist. "They're circling the wagons."

"What?"

"It's an expression from frontier times in America," Blaise said, putting up one arm to ward off the irate raven, which still urged them towards the ship. "The settlers used to travel across the land in wagon train convoys and if they got threatened, they drove them into a circle formation to defend themselves better."

"There's no one here," she said. "So who's moving those ships?"

"And what are they protecting?"

Sunni shook her fist at the squawking raven. "You aren't helping us with this decision, raven! Anything could be out there! How do we know it's safe?"

The bird glared at her and without any further sound flew out towards the cluster of ships, vanishing into the dark.

"Now what?" She pushed back a damp hank of hair.

Blaise looked down at the torn sleeves of Munro's fancy shirt. He wondered what was going on in the Mariner's Chamber and silently prayed that the untrustworthy spirit photographer could keep the flame lit long enough for them to get Lorimer and leave.

Sunni interrupted his prayer. "Listen!"

The distant sound of men's voices hummed from somewhere behind them, echoing up from the canal paths and lanes.

"People are coming," she said.

"We could hide in one of these houses and watch them, see what they do next," he suggested.

"Okay."

They began moving rapidly towards the nearest houses but the raven stormed in from the sea and dropped something flat and white in front of Sunni. Bemused, she picked it up.

Blaise watched her face drop with a mix of surprise and wistfulness as she rubbed the piece of parchment paper between her thumb and forefinger.

She turned it so he could see. It was a simple, yet astonishing, sketch of a girl's face with a looping signature below it. The face was Sunni's and yet it was not. Clearly she had not posed for it so it must have been done from memory. The artist had made her look older, with the solemn expression of a marble statue. And the signature made Blaise's blood rise.

"It's from Marin," Sunni said. "The raven brought this from one of those ships."

Corvo's eldest apprentice was the last person Blaise wanted Sunni to cross paths with again, especially since the guy seemed to have a pretty good recall of what she looked like. What was *that* all about?

"Yeah, well, he must have been pulled in from Arcadia too," said Blaise sourly. "Unless he's a clone."

"A clone wouldn't be able to draw me from memory," she said.

"No," he admitted.

"You're annoyed."

"I'm not. Can we go now?" It was no good losing his cool over something like this when there were life and death issues at hand. But a little part of him still didn't like Marin, who was older, handsomer, had an Italian accent, was a better artist than Blaise and, most importantly, Sunni had fancied him when they were in Arcadia.

The raven herded them towards a ship whose hull was hardly visible, as it had been so superimposed with elements from Arcadia. There was no need for a ramp. A winding piece of a lane had merged with the dock.

It was as Blaise ushered Sunni ahead of him that he saw distant torchlights back on shore. He scurried on board and hid, his heart thumping. The raven flew down to the dock and pulled the ropes from the moorings with its beak. As if the vessel had no anchor, it began sailing purposefully out to sea, leaving two more ships to follow. The raven flew to the next ship and prepared to free it.

Blaise watched a phalanx of sailors march through the gap between the Amsterdam houses, torches and pikes in hand. Soranzo was at the front. A rangy and heavily bearded Angus walked a step or two behind. Blaise's lip twisted at the sight of this man who'd caused him, Sunni and Dean so much trouble inside *The Mariner's Return* last winter. And now he was back helping Soranzo find Corvo.

Sunni was at his side, still clutching her portrait. "Is *that* Angus?"

"Yeah," he said. "Makes a good werewolf."

"Why is he risking seeing Fausto Corvo again?" she asked. "Corvo will just find some other punishment for him."

"I thought the same thing," said Blaise. "But Corvo's magic's all over the place now. I mean, look around us. Stuff from Arcadia's under-layers is all mashed up with this ship." He hesitated before adding, "And where is Corvo with this happening right under his nose?"

"If we find Marin, maybe he'll be able to tell us."

"He'd better," Blaise muttered. They climbed up the partial lane, passing half a barrow of loaves and the right side of the baker selling them.

"I remember seeing some of these faces when we were transported inside *The Mariner's Return*," said Sunni. "It seems so long ago."

"I was pretty excited the first time I saw them," he said, pausing to look at a finely dressed lady.

"Dean wasn't."

Blaise laughed for what seemed like the first time in ages. "Dean. What a guy. I think he's the smartest of us, staying out of all this after he left the painting last winter."

The ship gently glided into the mist, taking its place in the circle with the others. Tendrils of fog curled around the crooked windows of the medieval walls that had grown out of the hull.

They picked their way to the ship's bow, where a fountain now stood on cobbles, and peered out at the water. It was hard to see what the mist was hiding, other than something dark and vertical in the distance.

Looking ghostly in the thick fog, their neighbouring ships bobbed up and down. The sea lapped at the hulls, making hollow thudding sounds below. The raven had not shown itself again.

Sunni went quiet. Blaise saw she was studying her portrait and he left her to it. He hung on to a lattice of ropes, staring into the mist for something, anything, to show up. When it came it was the person he least wanted to see.

Corvo's apprentice, Marin, materialised from the mist on the next ship, like a spider climbing in the rigging. When the two vessels bumped, Blaise watched him in profile, sweeping his arm in front of him and touching his fingertips together, mouthing words at the same time. With each movement, the two ships were woven together, moving up and down as one. When his magic was done, the young man let his arms rest.

Moments later he descended the ropes and jumped in front of them, gesturing wildly in Blaise's face. "What is this evil you have brought now? It is ruining my master's work!"

At first Blaise was speechless. But he wasn't going to let Marin get to him.

He lifted his chin and said in a clear voice, "We're trying to rescue my teacher and leave so there will be no more trouble."

"And I am trying to rescue *my* teacher!" shouted Marin, his amber eyes bulging.

"What? Where is he?" Blaise asked, but the apprentice cut him off, holding up a shaking finger to silence him.

"I will tell you NOTHING!" he said. "You are like Pandora, opening the box and letting evil out! Why? Why could you not leave us alone?"

The ninja threw his mask across the Mariner's Chamber.

"Calm down," Mandy said, regarding Dean's bare face with a look of disgust. "I still can't believe I let you dance with me!"

"You'll get over it," said Dean.

"Maybe. Now start talking," she said, adjusting Lexie's position in her arms.

"I'll tell you everything, but first let's get this guy off the floor," said Dean. "That's his cat, by the way."

Mandy seemed unperturbed by the phantoms swirling about and stroked Lexie's head as she tried to put her on the ground. "He's not taking very good care of her. She's scared out of her wits. Look, the poor thing's still clinging to me."

"Aren't *you* scared?" Dean tried to prop Munro up, but the man kept falling back like a sack of potatoes, so he took him by one shoulder and gestured for Mandy to do the same on the other side.

"Not really. These spirits are too busy with each other to bother with me," she said, matter of fact, and picked up the shredded Ouija board from the floor.

"Spirits, it's time to go now," Munro repeated under his breath. "You really must go back to the other side immediately."

"Fat chance of that," said Mandy, grabbing him under the other armpit and pulling him towards the bench. "You called them out on Halloween night and there are too many to handle. They're a right rough crew as well and I reckon you're a bit over-sensitive."

"Can't you say something to them?" asked Dean, shuddering as the invisible apparitions tangled with each other.

"And end up like this guy? Best thing is to ignore them and concentrate on Sunni."

"And Blaise," he said, shoving the house keys, wallets, sketchbook and phones further down the bench so they could lay Munro out.

"Blaise is in there too?"

"That's Sunni's wallet and phone, and those keys, so the other stuff is probably his," he said, opening the sketchbook. "Yeah, his name's in here."

With a huge effort, the pair hoisted Munro up and got him settled.

Mandy picked Lexie back up and cuddled her. "And you've been spying on them because? Give it to me in a nutshell please."

"I was bored." Dean shrugged and screwed up his mouth.

"You bored? With all those games you play constantly?" she snorted.

"I knew Sunni was up to something. She's been sneaking around with Blaise behind my mum's back. I thought I'd follow them and see what they got up to. But last night something happened and Sunni got all secretive. Even more than usual."

"Ouija board," said Mandy knowingly, ducking one of the spirits who came too close. "That's how we met Lady Ishbel."

Dean nodded. "And I heard my mum talking to yours on the phone this morning about what happened. The next thing I knew, Sunni was off to Blackhope Tower this afternoon. So I followed her."

"And she was in here with Blaise," Mandy suggested.

"Yeah. I sneaked up here earlier looking for them. But this guy caught me at the door," he said, jerking his thumb at Munro. "Then I tried again and heard him telling Sunni and Blaise about this Oculus thing and it sounded fishy. So I sneaked back again tonight."

"Is it supposed to be projecting right on top of that painting?" Mandy moved closer to the Oculus and squinted at the light beaming across the chamber. "The picture's all messed up."

She jumped away from the magic lantern when one of the phantoms lowered its weapon and flew towards the projection, hovering around its perimeter. Two others joined him and then the rest, all nosing around the sides of the painting like sharks circling. And then one by one, they vanished into the Oculus's light.

Chapter 20

All through Marin's tirade Sunni had stood silently, her mouth hanging open. He was angry at what was happening and she didn't blame him, but she thought they'd become friends and allies in Arcadia.

He turned to her with a frown. "You like your portrait, Sunniva? If I had drawn a dog would you have come?"

Sunni wanted to pitch the portrait sketch right into the sea. When she thought of all the times when they were together inside *The Mariner's Return* and she had wished he'd say her name just once. Now she wished he hadn't.

"The drawing could have been of anything. It had your signature on it, Marin," she said carefully. "That was all I needed as proof that it was sent by a *friend*."

"I see. And now you are here, as a *friend*, you will undo the harm you have caused."

"I want that more than anything. But how?"

"Go back to your world and extinguish the Oculus's flame," Marin said.

"We can't leave our teacher here." Blaise crossed his arms over his chest. "Soranzo has him."

Marin gritted his teeth in a disbelieving smile. "Can't?

"Blaise is right," said Sunni. "When we have Mr Bell, we'll leave immediately. And we don't have much time!"

Before Marin could direct any more rage at them, a call came from somewhere in the mist. The voice was a young man's. Another younger voice answered and repeated the call.

Marin stopped and listened. His angry face went slack with dismay. He called back in Italian and climbed back into the rigging without explanation.

Sunni dropped the sketch and ran to Blaise's side. She held his elbow tight and said, "What Munro did isn't our fault."

"No," he replied. "But we played around with the Oculus and started all this."

"We weren't to know what would happen," she said.

"I think we had a pretty good idea since Corvo's magic is involved!" he said sharply, then mumbled, "Sorry."

But she was looking past him at something.

The mist had thinned slightly in the centre of the circle. Something monumentally tall and black spiked out of the sea like a skeleton's bony finger. Sunni tried to make it out against the indigo of the sky but the mist closed back over it.

"What was that?" she whispered.

"Huh?"

"There was something out there. It's gone now."

"Look, Sunni, I get that Marin's protective," Blaise said. "He's always been Corvo's attack dog. Nothing's changed except we're on his enemy list again."

"Unless we find a way to get Mr B and get out."

"Yeah," he said. "Like we can do that from here."

"Hey! Do you want me to start pointing fingers at

the person who wanted to follow the raven? Because it wasn't me."

"No, not until *Marin* drew your picture."

"Look what he's done within two minutes of us being here. He's got us fighting." She turned away and started walking. "Maybe you should take your dad's advice. Climb your imaginary hill and look at your problems a different way."

"Sunni…" he began in a pleading way.

But she shook her head and said, "I need a minute alone, all right?"

Sunni walked through the mid-section of the ship, trying to calm down. As she explored, she recognised a few characters from the top layer of *The Mariner's Return*. Unlike those in the living under-layers of Arcadia, these painted people were frozen and unmoving. They stood by their bread and vegetable stalls, and the sight of the painted food made Sunni wish she'd eaten something before she'd come out. They were probably starting the buffet at the party by now. She forced herself to move her thoughts elsewhere. Maybe Blaise's dad was right and she should find a high place to look down on her problems too.

A wall and two-storey staircase from *The Mariner's Return* had bled through and now grew out from the mainmast. The staircase was narrow and had no railing but it was they highest thing she could climb. Fed up with tripping over her long gown, she sat on the bottom step and ripped it upwards from the hem to the knee. With a hard tug, she ripped the cloth horizontally and it came away in a long strip. She wound this round her hair to keep it back and resolutely climbed the stairs.

When Sunni reached the top she clung to a crooked window in the wall and looked out. The perch was dizzyingly high. The mist dissipated here and, though she could barely see the other ships they were tethered to, she had a clear view of Amsterdam. The skyline had changed radically since they arrived. From a flat, silent city under a full moon, it had transformed into a place with hills and woods, hedges and islands, under rising and setting suns.

The quay was empty. The other two ships were now gone too. And there was no sign of Soranzo and his sailors.

Sunni hung over the window frame, trying to think of a way out of this predicament. She was aware of grunting and muttering sounds coming from the misty air nearby. A shape was in the next ship's rigging, very high. The figure was spread-eagled like a star and she knew in an instant that it was Marin. Every few moments he would bring one arm down as if he was throwing a stone at the ground and exclaim something in a language she could not understand. And then he'd go still.

Suddenly Marin peered intently at the water below and shook his head in disbelief.

Sunni followed the direction of his gaze at the open water beyond the mist. When she saw what floated into view, she covered her mouth in worried surprise. One of the ships that had left after theirs was slowly sailing past and it was full of sailors with lanterns.

Soranzo stood in a circle of them, leaning lazily against a long pike with something stuck on its tip.

Sunni's heart sank.

From his high perch Marin threw his arm down even more sharply, and as he did so, he conjured up a wave that pushed Soranzo's ship back for just a moment. Their enemy only laughed and called out something scornful in Italian that echoed across the water.

When his ship had drawn very close, Soranzo held his pike up as if to show Marin what was on it. When Sunni realised that the limp black thing stuck to its point was a raven, she had to swallow hard and look away. Was this the same messenger bird that had guided them and set loose their ship?

A hoarse *psst* came from the bottom of the stairs. Blaise climbed up after her, his eyes earnest with apology and curiosity. When he got to the top, she shushed him before he could say anything and pointed at Soranzo and at Marin hanging in the rigging.

Angus lurked behind Soranzo, looking restless. He muttered something and his new ally shrugged.

"I call out to Fausto Corvo!" Soranzo bellowed. "I call him by the spirits of all the men who died trying to find him. I will have vengeance in their names! And I must at last know the *true* location of the three enchanted paintings."

"I can tell you that if you'll listen." Angus pointed in the direction of the ring of ships. "Corvo has them in his workshop in the stone sea stack behind that fog. I've seen them with my own eyes!"

Sunni glanced behind her. Was that what she had glimpsed a few moments before? There was no sign now of the sheer-sided needle of rock sticking out of the sea, as it had in Arcadia.

Soranzo gave Angus a dismissive look. "One of Corvo's tricks to put hunters off the scent. And you believed it."

There was a disturbance on Soranzo's ship as the air churned above the crew's heads. Even he looked alarmed as, one by one, the seven spirits from the Mariner's Chamber assembled on deck around him, visible to everyone.

"Who – or what – are they?" Blaise whispered, aghast.

"I don't know!" Sunni chewed her thumb anxiously and scanned the deck.

Soranzo gazed at the ghostly newcomers in astonishment. Whether or not he recognised their corrupted faces, Sunni couldn't tell, but he acknowledged them with a bow.

She saw by Marin's rigid outline that this development stunned him. He sat motionless and seemed unable to come up with any other magic to hold back his master's enemy.

Soranzo rolled his head from side to side, a strange jubilation in his face. "My band of followers is growing!"

"This is all we need," said Blaise. "Do you see Mr B anywhere on their ship?"

"No," said Sunni. "And now we've got to get past those *things* to find him."

Soranzo seemed to have grown taller and more robust since the spirits arrived.

"Fausto Corvo," he called, sounding relaxed and confident. "I see only your minions in the rigging but I know you can hear me. No doubt you are hiding in your lair, desperately trying to correct all that has gone wrong with your sorcery!"

He turned to his sailors and commanded them to laugh. They fell about, but none more than Angus whose grin shone from his darkly tanned and rough-bearded face.

"You never thought about what could happen if someone was intelligent enough to steal the Oculus and point its light at your painting," Soranzo went on. "My spies learned of an object on its way to Prague. That was nothing unusual, but it was to be delivered to Emperor Rudolf himself, and you were the man who sent it. I decided to have my lieutenants intercept the object on its journey. Imagine my delight when I obtained your Oculus shadow lantern and the glass pictures!"

Sunni noticed that Angus tensed at this news and watched Soranzo intently.

"It took me some time to work out that I could enter each shadowland and how to return. You must have sent directions to the Emperor separately, so he would know exactly what to do with the lantern, but as he never received the Oculus, they were useless." Soranzo was enjoying his monologue, no doubt hoping that Corvo was squirming somewhere as he listened. "You wanted to tell him your pathetic story about running from Venice and Prague, making me out to be a monster! I have never understood why you wanted Emperor Rudolf to have your paintings. He already had castles full of paintings and jewels and treasures. Why should *he* have everything?" He clenched his fist and shook it at the air. "And in the end you had no time to see the Emperor. Poor Corvo!"

He began to seethe and sway. "In these projections your doubles waited fruitlessly for Emperor Rudolf to use the Oculus and come inside so they could tease him about where your three paintings are hidden. Because you knew he enjoyed curiosities, you also embedded clues in the shadowlands. I have seen the coded names on ships and signs. Your doubles had a cipher disc for Rudolf to help him break the code!"

Blaise murmured, "Cipher disc?"

"The last clone said something about a cipher," whispered Sunni.

Soranzo chucked the pike with the raven's body on it at Angus, who just managed to grab it. Soranzo took something small and rectangular out of his doublet and waved it with his free hand. "Answer me another question, Corvo, when you have enough courage to show yourself! This is the *fourth* glass picture. And I have been in its shadowland."

Sunni heard Blaise let out a 'whoa' under his breath and she was just as surprised.

"In the fourth shadowland, Corvo, you sailed from Amsterdam to London," the man shouted. "The long satchels containing your paintings were not with you on that ship. What did you do with them? Where are they?"

"What just happened?" Dean stared at the beam of light where the seven spirits had vanished. "It's gone quiet all of a sudden."

"You've got me there," said Mandy, rubbing the scratches on her arm. "It's a lot calmer without them though." She looked down at Lexie, who was contentedly nuzzling her neck. Her owner, Munro, was half unconscious on the bench, still occasionally mumbling orders for the phantoms to leave.

Mandy smiled and called out in a sweet voice, "Lady Ishbel, are you here? You can come out." The air whooshed around them and Lexie followed it with her green-golden eyes, unperturbed now. "Oh! You certainly are here. Can you tell me what just happened?" Her face went serious as she listened. "My goodness! The painting has opened up and the other spirits have gone inside to find Fausto Corvo?" She raised her eyebrows at Dean, whose jaw dropped. "And you're going in to fight against them with who? Mar-Mar-Marin…"

Dean scowled in disbelief at this unwelcome name.

"Okay," said Mandy. "If you see our friends in there, Sunni and Blaise, please help them too?" A sharp gust of wind snarled around her and she jumped.

As the whirlwind met the beam of the Oculus, a slender young woman with long wild hair materialised in front of them. She turned, in her puffed-out dress, to give them a fiery look and marched into the light.

Chapter 21

At Soranzo's speech, the seven spectres quivered and raised their weapons, which prompted the sailors to do the same. Their leader stamped about holding the fourth glass slide up in both hands like a hard-won prize. His band of followers went wild.

Blaise watched them with a stone-hard dread in the pit of his stomach. He touched the round metal object in his pocket to make sure it was still safe. Was it the cipher disc Soranzo mentioned?

The spectres danced in the air like flying devils and the sailors whooped among them. But Blaise's eyes were glued to Angus. He was making a good show of support, applauding Soranzo, but his hairy face was sombre.

"Angus doesn't look happy," he whispered to Sunni.

"Who cares?" she hissed. "He's Soranzo's problem now."

Yeah, Blaise thought, *unless we cross paths with him again*.

Soranzo put the fourth Oculus slide back in his doublet and barked an order. His ship vanished in the mist.

Marin sprang to life, throwing down spells one after another. The mist suddenly broke up and blew out to sea, revealing Corvo's younger apprentices Dolphin and Zorzi on two other ships, sweeping their arms in the same way as Marin. Blaise could now see the entire ring of twelve brightly coloured ships magically tethered together from bow to stern. In the centre of the floating circle was the sea stack, a pointed black rock in the dark.

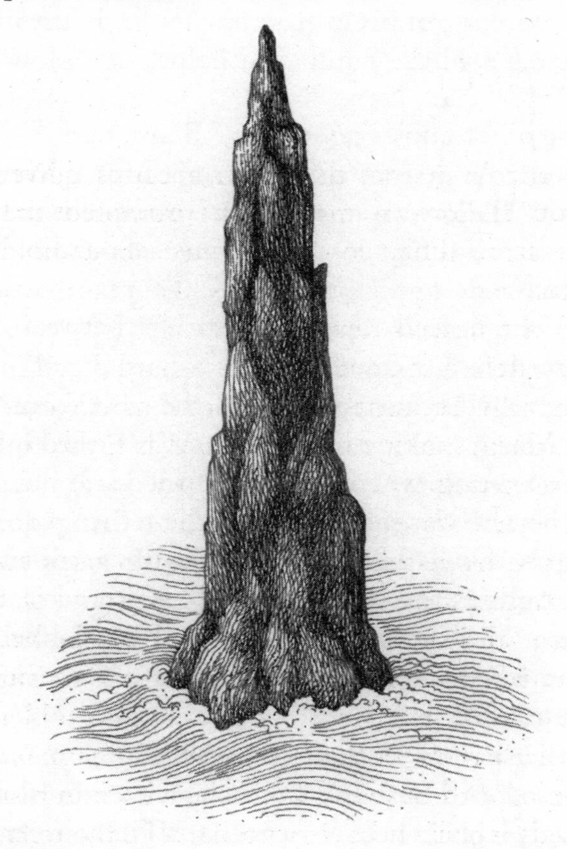

Slowly the tethered ships groaned and began revolving like a huge merry-go-round. The apprentices were straining hard, as if they were physically pushing the vessels, when a whirlwind came out of the sky and whistled through the rigging.

Ahhhhh. The wind passed round Blaise's head as if it were checking him out, then gave Sunni a ringing blast, sending her hair straight up and nearly knocking her off the staircase. He got his arm across her back just in time.

"That was Ishbel!" Sunni said helplessly. "How did she get in?"

"Those other ghosts got in too," Blaise said.

"I wonder. When we did the Ouija board, Mandy told us that on Halloween the barriers come down between worlds," said Sunni, "so now spirits can cross into the projection too."

"Yeah," he agreed. "And the barriers between Corvo's worlds are already messed up."

The whirlwind gusted towards the neighbouring ship and sent Marin shaking in the rigging. He cried out, about to lose his footing, when the wind turned and hugged him close. When he was safe it pushed the tethered ships with an almighty howl. His face blank with surprise, Marin hung on tight as the ships revolved faster and faster. And powering it all from behind him was Lady Ishbel's spirit, taking human shape with her arms round his neck and her hair streaming.

"I can see her now," Blaise breathed.

"Me, too," said Sunni. "I hope she leaves me alone."

But Lady Ishbel's help came too late. The thirteenth boat, Soranzo's, had already attached itself to one of the ships in the circle like a parasitic insect. Sailors fastened ropes and scrambled aboard, jumping from ship to ship, roaring and laughing, while the spectres buzzed around them.

"Find Corvo and bring him to me!" Soranzo commanded.

As the ring of ships sped round and round, Blaise and Sunni clung to the window frame at the top of the staircase.

"Any ideas to get us out of here?" she gasped.

"I've got to get back down on the deck or I'm going to puke." He dropped to his knees and crawled down backwards, his shoulder close to the wall. Sunni shakily did the same until they staggered onto the deck, feeling about for anything solid to grab hold of.

She rolled into a corner, sheltered by part of a wall, and urged Blaise in. A couple of sailors were already stomping unsteadily through the ship, their weapons clattering.

"Fausto Corvo!" Soranzo's sonorous voice came from somewhere unnervingly close to them. "If this is the best sorcery your apprentices can conjure, we will soon be upon you! You are already finished."

Blaise nudged Sunni further into the corner, trying to block out her white figure with his darker clothes. Soranzo threaded his way across the deck like a victorious commander, taking hold of walls and ropes to keep him steady, and speaking to two spectres in Italian. They hovered around him, their hideous faces intent.

When they had met him before Soranzo had not looked unhinged, but he did now. There was something too wide and sparkly about the ice blue eyes, as if they had spent too long hunting for Corvo and his paintings. His hands twitched from too much grasping for riches and secrets.

Once Soranzo and the phantoms had vanished round the next wall, Blaise whispered, "Time to bail out of here. Soranzo's boat is only two ships down from us. If we can get to it, maybe we can untie it and sail it back to shore.

We're not that far out. Mr B might be on board too."

"How can we sail a ship by ourselves?" Then Sunni's eyes brightened. "If we could let Marin know we're trying to leave, maybe he'd use his magic to help us."

"The minute we call out to him, we're as good as caught."

"Okay, then we just go!"

With ears trained and eyes sharp, Blaise and Sunni inched out of their hiding place and crawled along the deck, which at times became a cobbled lane. They were going against the flow of the ships' movement, like walking backwards on a merry-go-round, and trying to watch out for enemies, when Sunni hissed, "Look up!"

Marin, with Lady Ishbel still clinging to him, took a sheet of parchment from inside his shirt and closed his eyes. He uttered something and a new raven zoomed out of the night. It whipped the parchment from his hand and carried it away, vanishing in the direction of the sea stack.

"Keep going," Blaise urged, unconvinced that Marin had the power to change anything. "It doesn't matter what he's doing. This is our chance to get off."

They crawled over the hull of their ship and climbed onto the next, which was just as cluttered with sections of buildings and unmoving people. It even had a few motionless cattle on the poop deck. Soranzo's sailors had spread out across the wheel of thirteen ships and Blaise could hear their voices on the other side of the sea stack.

"There's no one here." He was almost gleeful, even though he still felt as if he was going to be sick.

Sunni smiled hopefully and kept crawling. When they had reached the next tethered ship and could see Soranzo's vessel bobbing beside it, Blaise's heart was in his mouth. *Almost there.*

But as he made his next move, the dome of the sky lit up with a criss-crossing grid of lightning. Blaise rolled onto his back and pulled Sunni down beside him. The lightning bolts seemed to strike everywhere at once, emanating like fireworks from one dark source in the centre of the magic circle: the sea stack. But the tall stone tower had grown limbs and a head, morphing into the active shape of a bearded man. His fingers drew with lightning bolts, all ten fingers working simultaneously. Planets appeared high overhead and hundreds of constellations in the shapes of humans and animals.

The hands never stopped drawing, covering the sky with symbols and ciphers, mythical beasts and ancient goddesses, all cracking and sizzling into place. When the silhouette turned to work another part of the darkness, it showed its monumental face to them and Blaise shuddered in awe. This was a man-constellation, a network of blinking, moving stars that formed a face, hands and the outline of a body, but was completely wired in to the heavens. Even in this bizarre form, it could be none other than Fausto Corvo.

"Now what?" Mandy plonked herself down on the bench next to Munro.

The Mariner's Chamber was silent and dark, except for the Oculus's low beam. Dean was staring at the projection, trying to make out what was happening to it. Pieces of it were disappearing and other patches were appearing.

"Him." Dean pulled his attention away from the wall and pointed at Munro. "Time to sort this guy out."

He leaned over the spirit photographer and shook him by the lapels. Munro muttered and shook his head.

"Wake up," said Dean. "They're gone. Hear that? Gone."

But Munro was in a world of his own, his fingers drumming incessantly, as he murmured unintelligible words at no one in particular.

"I think he might be gone, too," said Mandy. "Maybe if you got those crazy glasses off him…"

Dean unhooked the clockwork spectacles from behind Munro's ears and examined them. "Violet-coloured lenses."

"Weird."

Munro's eyes were tightly shut, so Mandy leaned over and said in a gentle voice, "Mister, you're all right. The spirits have gone to the other side. Well, *another* side anyway."

Munro's eyes popped open and rolled around. He let out a gigantic sigh of relief and pinched the bridge of his nose hard with his thumb and forefinger. "Splitting headache."

Dean twirled the clockwork specs in his hand. "Maybe you need a new prescription."

"Put those down!"

"Okay, okay." He went to the Oculus's table and laid them down with care. "You're lucky we came in."

Munro sat up, still clutching his nose, and said sharply, "How did you get in here?"

"We have ways."

"Who knows about this?"

"Nobody. Our little secret," said Dean. "That's if you

tell us what happened to Sunni and Blaise."

"I haven't the slightest idea," said Munro.

"Really?" Dean snorted. "What were they doing in here this afternoon then? And tonight!"

Munro frowned. "I've been putting on shows for the public all day."

"But Sunni and Blaise came back here tonight," said Dean. "Didn't they?"

"You were the one spying at the door, weren't you?" Munro folded his arms across his chest. "I don't owe you any explanation."

"The sign outside says no one's allowed in and the door was locked," said Mandy, petting Lexie. "So how come Sunni and Blaise were here?"

Munro glanced at the Oculus, then the wall. Alarm crossed his face at the changes in the painting, but he said nothing.

"Well?" asked Dean, his mouth set in a line. "I've got time to wait for an answer."

"So have I," said Mandy.

"I haven't. I have a Halloween show to get ready for." Munro stood up and brushed down his leather coat. He glanced at his pocket watch, then picked up his hat, broken camera, glasses, the remains of the Ouija board and the indicator, and stuffed them in his pockets. He began to walk stiffly towards the door. "Come on, time for you to go."

A burst of lightning came from the projection on the wall and crackled in mid-air. As the Oculus's golden beam of light met the jagged pops of blue-white light, the atmosphere in the Mariner's Chamber shifted.

"What is that?" Dean jumped up and put his hands out to Munro, looking for answers. "Come on, you know what's going on!"

"No, I don't!" The spirit photographer's mouth hung slack as he hurried over to the Oculus and stared at the projection, which was now a flashing rectangle of changing shapes and marks. "I truly don't know what's going on."

"Your spirit friends are in there," said Mandy sarcastically, joining them at the table. "That projection opened up and they went in. We saw them. So what gives?"

"*You* saw them?" Munro covered his gaping mouth with his hand. "This… this is beyond me."

She gave him a scorching look as though this didn't surprise her.

The projection was now spitting blue-white bolts and the wall behind it began to throb. Hairline cracks radiated out from behind *The Mariner's Return*, running up to the ceiling and down to the floor. The painted ceiling beams shuddered and dust fell in a fine shower, lit up like a snow flurry by the Oculus's beam.

"My stepsister and my friend are in there!" Dean shouted, pointing at the chaotic maelstrom of symbols and signs on the wall, while looking in horror at the loosening beams overhead. "You'd better have an idea how to get her out, because I don't!"

Chapter 22

Fausto Corvo's stellar hands erased and redrew, changed and added to the panorama above them, seemingly oblivious to the people and creatures on the revolving wheel of ships below him. The sky was his celestial blackboard, covered in a formula of deep and strange complexity.

Sunni lay on her back next to Blaise, pressed to the deck. The ships were circling this manifestation of Corvo at a swift pace, making it difficult to move, but she was also mesmerised by what was taking place overhead.

"Are you all right?" she whispered.

"Not sure," Blaise answered. "I think my brain is about to overload with what's going on up there. The sky looks like all the maths problems I've ever seen in my whole life, with dragons and centaurs and astrology symbols thrown in."

"I recognise some of this stuff," she said in a low voice. "The walls of the palace in Arcadia were covered from top to bottom in these types of symbol. Corvo memorised all of them so that he could draw down the power of the stars to create living worlds from his paintings."

"It's code then, like DNA," Blaise said. "This is his drawing board and it looks like he's making some changes."

"We've got to go while we still can!" Sunni rolled onto her side and carefully got up on all fours. "I hope Ishbel slows down the wind power or we'll never get off this merry-go-round." She crawled a few feet and turned round. "Come on!"

"Um, Sunni…" Blaise was staring, open-mouthed, at Corvo's astral entity whose arms swept across the heavens, seemingly finished with its work. The whole dome sparkled as a million crystalline marks and symbols settled into a mind-boggling, heavenly mural.

Suddenly, over the city, a sun that had bled through from one of Arcadia's under-layers fell from the sky like a melting blob of orange sorbet and vanished. The gold and terra cotta surfaces of the medieval houses' walls began to be stripped away, layer by layer, from the ships' hulls, until all that was left were skeletal under-drawings. The colours came away in ribbons and sheets and the charcoal drawings came apart like twigs, all caught up in Lady Ishbel's powerful whirlwind.

"Everything's coming apart!" Blaise said, scrambling to his hands and knees, ducking the flying swathes of colour.

"Let's go!" Sunni gasped, as she crawled under the belly of a stationary cow, whose brown and white hide flew off it, leaving just a sketch underneath. The charcoal lines burst apart like an explosion of bones and joined the tornado overhead.

One by one the crazy patchwork of houses, streets, motionless animals and inanimate people was being unravelled and sent by Corvo to where it belonged. The boat was returning to its original dark state, with several tall masts, billowing sails and high decks at front and back. She could just see Marin with Lady Ishbel, Dolphin and Zorzi, sentinels in their high perches watching their master undo his creations.

But where was Soranzo? *No time to find out*.

Feeling increasingly exposed, Sunni sought refuge behind one of the few remaining pieces of wall still attached to the main mast. Blaise was behind her, crawling on hands and knees.

She curled into a ball to avoid flying debris and rolled in behind the wall, only to bump into someone who was already hiding there. He grasped her shoulder with a powerful grip and pulled her backwards against his knees. Sunni grimaced as she fought to get away. Her captor stank to high heaven.

"Sunni," Angus said sharply. "Relax. I'm not going to hurt you."

Blaise, his face burning with a look of utter contempt, hurled himself at them and started punching Angus's arms and shoulders.

Angus batted Blaise away with a sinewy brown arm and held out his finger in warning. "Truce! I'm not your enemy here."

"Oh, really?" Blaise sputtered, looking ready to pounce again. "What about your offer to help Soranzo *crush* us? Because we have *unfinished business*!"

"All right, so you overheard me lying," said Angus, his sour breath close to Sunni's ear.

"Nothing new there," she said, squirming at the sight of Angus's dirty fingers holding her fast.

"Yes, Sunni, I had to lie." Angus released her with a push towards Blaise. "Go on. I told you, I'm not here to hurt anyone."

"Tigers don't change their stripes," she spat, taking in his long shaggy hair and bleached, shredded clothing. "You told Soranzo that your own cousin means nothing to you."

Angus screwed up his bearded face as if in pain. "You've got me all wrong. Seriously, all I want is to get out of Corvo's crazy world and go home – *with* Lorimer. I'll turn myself in to the police when I get back, even if I go to jail for knocking out that guard at Blackhope Tower. Hey, at least I'll get three meals a day."

"What about the magical paintings?" Blaise asked suspiciously. "You'd do anything to get hold of them. You're as bad as Soranzo."

He shrugged. "Right now, I'd take being in a jail back home over all the magical paintings in the world."

"Uh-huh," said Blaise, pulling Sunni away by the shoulder. "Good luck."

"No wait, you've got to believe me," Angus exclaimed, getting to his knees and putting his hands together as if in prayer. "I have a proposal."

"Get lost," Blaise replied scornfully, urging Sunni to move as the wall Angus had leaned against began to disassemble and shoot off into the wind.

"I guess I can't blame you. The thing is, I know where Lorimer is and I want to get us both out." He glanced around as their sheltering wall came away from the mast and flew off, leaving the trio sitting on the empty deck. "And if we don't move fast, I'll get sucked back onto the island Corvo banished me to."

Blaise stopped dead. "Where is Mr Bell?"

"He's here," said Angus. "But he's a bit beaten up and

out of it. I don't know if he could figure out the way back. That's where you'd come in." He hung his head. "But it's okay, you go on ahead and save yourselves. I'll get Lorimer home somehow."

"This is garbage!" Blaise laughed bitterly. "Where's Soranzo? Waiting to jump us the minute we help you?"

Sunni kept quiet, watching every change of expression on the man's face.

"No, he's over there." Angus pulled himself up and fought against the wind to reach the railing overlooking the centre of the magic circle of ships. On one of the furthest ships, Soranzo and his followers were gathered, defiantly holding their blazing lanterns in the air against Corvo's celestial display. "And so is Lorimer."

"I can't see him," said Blaise, as he and Sunni clung to the hull.

"Well, pal," said Angus, "if you can't see him then I must be lying again, eh?" He turned his back on them and began pulling himself along the railing.

"Would you take an oath that you're not lying?" Sunni asked quickly, ignoring Blaise's furious glance at her. "On Mr Bell's life?"

"Of course," he replied.

Blaise jumped in. "What about an extra oath on your pigs' graves?"

Angus's shoulders slumped. "What do you know about my pigs?"

"They were taken by predators from Arcadia," Sunni answered, astonished to see the man's stricken face. "But it was quick. I don't think they suffered."

Angus ran a filthy hand over his eyes. "I raised them from piglets on my island. It was the best thing I ever did in my life. If you want an oath on that, pal, you've got it." He continued along the railing, head bowed.

Sunni expected a harsh comment from Blaise but nothing came. He was staring after Angus and she knew he was weighing things up. Without a word, he nodded and set off after him.

"Changed your mind?" Angus asked when Sunni and Blaise caught up and they climbed onto the next vessel.

"Not a hundred per cent," said Blaise. "That's up to you."

The tornado of torn colours and broken sketches churned in the dark above their heads, now pulling chunks out of the city. The green of the hedge mazes and the ochre of island sands flew over the sea and joined in, circulating higher and higher, courtesy of Lady Ishbel, who had not moved an inch from Marin's side.

"You think Ishbel's recognised me?" Angus's brow was furrowed as he looked up. "There was some bad blood between us in Arcadia. I'm surprised she hasn't launched me into the ozone layer yet."

"There's still time," said Sunni with a sniff. "But I think Ishbel's found the person she had the most unfinished business with."

They struggled along the length of six empty ships, shouting above the wind and keeping an eye out for sailors and spectres, but went unhindered. When they got close, they could see that Soranzo's ship was still surrounded in a bright flurry of deconstructed colours and drawings.

As one sailor ran across Soranzo's deck, his tanned

skin and rough clothes were unwound from his body like a mummy being unwrapped. The drawing of his figure was not much more complicated than a stick man and it blew away as if it had never existed.

"Corvo's taking out the enemy troops," said Angus, climbing onto Soranzo's chaotic ship. "Excellent."

"Ready?" Blaise gave Sunni a grim smile and she nodded.

Soranzo's vessel sighed with the last breaths of the vanishing sailors. Sunni shielded her face from the storm of flying materials and tried to keep up with Angus, who was edging along the side of the ship towards the bow.

Above the whirling colours she saw Soranzo's motionless figure on the top deck facing the sea stack. He talked non-stop, a frozen smile on his face, even though his sailors were being undone all around him.

"How's he keeping so steady?" Sunni muttered as she tried to stay on her feet.

"No idea. It's us I'm worried about. I'm going after Angus. You stay up here and keep an eye on things." Blaise pulled her into a dark spot under the top deck and hurried below through a small door.

Sunni huddled there, the force of the moving ship keeping her rigid against the wall. She was aware of Soranzo's voice growing louder as the wind carried the remains of his sailors up and away. The decks began to clear and she could once again make out the shapes of the other twelve boats moving swiftly round the sea stack.

"Fausto Corvo," Soranzo called. "I have waited hundreds of years to find you. You have thwarted me at every turn, hiding behind your apprentices, leaving puzzles to mislead me."

Corvo's silhouette in the sky seemed to pause for a moment and then continued surveying its work.

"You can easily crush me now," shouted Soranzo. "I have nothing left but my loyal followers from beyond the grave. So why do you not strike me down?" He laughed long and hard, sending a chill down Sunni's spine. "Stop hiding behind your sorcery, Corvo! Come and fight me like an honourable man, face to face."

To her surprise, Corvo's huge form folded in its arms and head and shrank back into the pointed sea stack. A raven belted out from its darkness and flew straight to Soranzo. In its beak was a sheet of parchment.

Alarmed that she couldn't see, Sunni sneaked to the middle of the deck and found a new hiding space behind a barrel, just as Blaise and Angus burst from below with Lorimer Bell between them. The teacher's face was bruised and he limped, but he gave her a pained smile. Sunni nearly burst with relief at seeing him and was ready to run over, but he held his hand out in a warning to stay still. Blaise and Angus sat him in a sheltered corner and moved to Sunni's side.

Blaise let out a breath. "He's all right."

The seven phantoms hovered over Soranzo, diverting Lady Ishbel's whirlwind. Each held a lantern, creating a ring of lights around him.

The raven dropped the parchment into the circle of wraiths. When it had drifted to the ground, the paper shook violently and the figure of Fausto Corvo sprang from it fully formed, his eyes flashing. He was dressed head to toe in black with a slender rapier in each hand.

Out of the corner of her eye, Sunni saw the three apprentices scramble down from the rigging to the main deck and hang onto the hull with anxious faces. Lady Ishbel still floated behind Marin, her arms tightly about his neck and a protective expression on her spirit face.

"Signore," Corvo said. With a formal bow, he tossed one of the weapons to Soranzo, who caught it one-handed in mid-air.

"English, signore," replied Soranzo, sweeping the rapier back and forth so it could taste the air. He nodded down at the main deck. "I wish them to hear the answers from your own lips before you die."

Corvo gave Sunni, Blaise and Angus a swift, dark glance and held the blade vertical in front of his ebony eyes before lowering it with a stiff flourish.

Soranzo briefly held his before his ice-blue eyes and the enemies assumed the *en garde* pose, rapiers extended. The weapons' two tips touched for a moment, then exploded in a flash of silver. As the two men danced around each other, thrusting and parrying, the spectres grinned. Above them, the flow of colours, marks, skins and other elements of Corvo's Arcadian underworlds continued as they were pulled back to where they belonged. The sky over Amsterdam was littered with flying shapes wrenched from the canals, sea and reclaimed earth of the city. And high above the entire soaring mass, the celestial drawing board glittered ominously.

"You did not understand the Oculus's fourth shadowland, Soranzo," Corvo grunted as he climbed backwards down the ladder and jumped onto the main deck. The seven spirits followed with their lanterns and set them down on the deck and on barrels. The flames hardly flickered, despite the wind.

Soranzo clattered down after him and darted sideways like a crab towards his adversary. "There was nothing to understand," he said through gritted teeth. "You sailed for London without the paintings."

"The answer was there all along!" Corvo smiled. "If you had been able to see it!"

The other man's face was outraged. "You did hide the three lost paintings in the fourth shadowland then?"

Corvo laughed out loud and with a quick slash of his rapier slit open Soranzo's doublet. Before his adversary could respond, he skewered the wooden frame of the fourth Oculus slide and pulled it away. As Corvo triumphantly raised the rectangle high in the air, everything went black.

Chapter 23

When the Oculus's flame went out, Munro barked, "No! No, the flame can't go out!" He fumbled about in the dark amidst the sound of plaster crackling and raining to the stone floor in small chunks. "Beam that torch here!"

Dean found the white-faced spirit photographer with his torchlight. "What do we do now?"

"I have to get that flame lit or they're not coming back!" Munro lunged towards the supplies on the table and knocked over the small bottle of oil. It fell with a thump, and a greasy pool began forming on the ground. He set it upright with a grimace and fished a handful of drenched wicks from it, his hand glistening in the light. "Open the magic lantern's door!"

"Hold the torch," Dean commanded Mandy, who quickly set Lexie down. She trained the light on the back of the Oculus and Dean yanked the door open. The spent wick spewed out a smelly curl of smoke and he coughed, brushing it away. "Now what?"

"Is there any oil in the pan?"

"Not much."

Munro slipped through the mess on the floor and pushed Dean out of the way. His hand shook so much as he tried to pour fresh oil into the Oculus that Mandy exclaimed,

"You can't even get your hand in there! Let Dean have a go!"

Dean glared at him. "Come on!" He took the bottle and kept his own hand still enough to pour a full amount into the oil container.

"Wick." Munro thrust the wet wicks at him and Dean teased one out. "Lay it in the oil and light it."

His own hand quaking now, Dean managed to get the wick into place.

"Matches," said Munro.

"Yeah? Where are they?" Dean nearly exploded as he searched around. "You were supposed to be looking after this, weren't you?"

Munro crouched awkwardly on the floor, feeling around in the oil slick.

"Here." Mandy pushed the small matchbox towards Dean. "Right on the table."

Swallowing hard, he struck his match again and again.

"I can do that," offered Munro.

"You've done enough already," muttered Dean as the match burst into flame. With one touch of it, the wick flowered into its familiar golden light. The projection returned, a mass of colours and shapes twisting and morphing before their eyes.

Dean turned to Munro, raging. "What did you mean they can't get out if the flame goes dead? How do you know that?"

"We found out how it works today, by accident," said Munro. "Sunni and Blaise have been in and out of two other projections and now they're trying to rescue Lorimer

Bell. He sneaked in behind my back. As long as the flame is on, they can all get out." He glanced at the wall. "That is, as long as we can see them."

"What do you mean?" asked Mandy.

"The minute they appear in that projection on the wall, someone has to kill the flame so they can be transported back. But something's gone wrong ever since I aimed the Oculus on the painting."

"What did you do that for?" Dean exclaimed.

Munro pinched the bridge of his nose again. "It's a long story."

"I'll bet," said Mandy disdainfully. "And then you were swamped by those spirits, weren't you?"

Suddenly, the Mariner's Chamber ceiling shook with a strange wind. A scratching noise came from the ancient wooden beams decorated with painted mermaids, dolphins and other odd sea creatures. Dean shone the light upwards and gasped. The beams were rapidly becoming dislodged.

The floor shifted slightly under their feet, and without waiting a moment more Mandy dropped the torch on the table, scooped Lexie up in her arms and ran through the dark to the door.

"We need help," she murmured, skidding out of the Mariner's Chamber and making her way blindly down the corridor.

"Yeah, and who do you know that can help with this?" Dean yelled after her, but she was already gone. He gave Munro a warning look. "Don't even think about following her. You're sticking it out here and getting them back, no matter what! Where are the keys to this place? Come on!"

Munro forlornly pulled his keys from his trouser pocket and, before he knew it, Dean had locked the Mariner's Chamber from the inside.

At that moment, Blackhope Tower shuddered as if an earthquake had rocked its foundations.

When Mandy got to the first-floor level of the spiral staircase, there were so many shocked guests leaving the fancy dress party that she was blocked in the narrow passage. She finally pushed through and made for the Great Hall against the tide of people cowering and shielding their heads, including Mrs Gordon who shouted directions no one was heeding.

Another tremor made the castle sway and there was a collective cry from the spiral staircase. As she ran into the nearly empty Great Hall, she collided with James and Iona. Lexie sprang from her arms and Mandy yelped, "Catch her!"

"That's Munro's cat," said Iona. "Where is he?"

"Upstairs," Mandy gasped, flailing about for Lexie, who had hidden under a table. "Help me!"

"Where upstairs?" James glanced nervously around him as the floor shuddered again. The Great Hall was covered in a fine coating of plaster dust from the network of fine cracks in the vaulted ceiling and the jack o' lantern blazed brighter than seemed possible.

"The Mariner's Chamber," she answered and hunted among the few remaining guests for her parents. But there was no sign of them. "Got to find my dad!"

"Everyone's gone outside," said James. "And we should too!"

"But Sunni," Mandy breathed. "And Blaise. And Mr Bell!"

"What about them?" Iona shook Mandy's arm hard. "What are you talking about?"

But Mandy couldn't answer. She pointed in horror at the skeleton and witch silhouettes falling off the walls, revealing a growing network of cracks. At that moment two adults pushed their way through the crowds of fleeing guests and stood frozen at the sight.

It was Sunni's dad and stepmum.

Blaise heard a man's angry cry and the smash of glass hitting the deck in the dark. There was a momentary scuffle, but everything went quiet and he was overtaken by a tremendous sleepiness, as if all his systems were shutting down.

"No, no, no," Sunni whimpered. "Munro's let the Oculus's flame go out!" Her fingers grasped about for his and nearly crushed them.

"Sunni," he whispered, fighting with all his might against the creeping fatigue. "This might be it for us, so..."

He heard a sharp sob. "No."

"I-I have to tell you something. I've wanted to for a really long time but every time..." He yawned. "But something happens every time..."

"What?" She asked between sniffles, her voice fading.

Blaise was losing consciousness. He let go of Sunni's hand. "I really..."

The lanterns exploded into light and he felt like he'd been slapped awake. Sunni looked at him wide-eyed, waiting for him to finish his sentence, but there was no time. To his annoyance, he noticed Angus was smirking at him as if he knew what Blaise had been about to tell her.

The fourth glass slide lay shattered on deck and the seven spectres had Fausto Corvo surrounded, their axes, daggers and garrottes poised to strike. He held them off with his glinting rapier.

"Now you do not fight like a gentleman, signore," said Corvo, glancing at his three apprentices and then back at the ghosts of the spies and bounty hunters who had pursued him for so long. He brought his free arm down and the fearful whirlwind slowed somewhat, though it continued pulling debris from Amsterdam into its vortex high above.

"You have destroyed the fourth shadowland!" Soranzo drew the tip of his rapier through the broken glass. "If the enchanted paintings were hidden in it, they are gone." He slowly turned to Corvo, his pale eyes wild with disbelief. "And there is no reason to keep you alive."

Corvo was scornful. "I have not destroyed my paintings! They are not in any of the four shadowlands – nor are they with me in Arcadia."

Blaise's mouth dropped open and Angus muttered "What?" under his breath.

Soranzo swept his blade back and forth as if he were cutting his adversary in half. "Explain!"

"You may as well know, since you will never be able to

put your foul hands on them," said Corvo. "If you leave this shadowland, you will die immediately. Too many years have passed for you to survive."

"I know this." Soranzo nodded at the scowling phantoms. "Like these brave men who ended up as skeletons on your labyrinth in the Mariner's Chamber."

"Yes, and you may haunt that chamber as these filthy spies no doubt have," said the magician. The wraiths roared at this insult and jangled their weapons.

Soranzo glared at Angus and pointed one shaking finger towards the sea stack. "This ruffian told me your three enchanted paintings are in that tower."

Angus glowered at this description.

"Only ordinary copies. It made no sense to leave the enchanted works there or inside glass pictures that *thieves* could steal." Corvo looked as though he was about to spit. "Instead, as you already know, I left coded messages about the paintings for His Imperial Majesty."

"Messages that I could not decipher without a cryptographer!"

Corvo gave a hard laugh. "What a terrible shame for you!"

"Your messages can go to the Devil!" Soranzo was so incensed that he nearly lunged at the artist. "Where did you hide the enchanted paintings?"

"They are somewhere under the Bright Ravens," Corvo replied enigmatically. "I left each one in a different place, but after four hundred years perhaps they have been moved."

"Under the Bright Ravens!" Soranzo seethed. "That is a riddle, not an answer."

"That is all I will say," said Corvo.

Under the Bright Ravens, Blaise repeated to himself.

"You're lying," said Soranzo, holding his blade up between his eyes and moving closer. "And I will have the truth from you."

"I speak the truth, Soranzo. Why should I lie? It is impossible for you to steal my paintings now. And that means you can never enter their enchanted under-layers and abuse the powers hidden there," said Corvo calmly. "You will leave this shadowland and die like any ordinary mortal. Or remain trapped here forever in darkness."

"No!" Soranzo lunged at Corvo and the spectres joined in.

The dark-eyed sorcerer's weapon was everywhere at once, holding off the vengeful spies and stabbing at his old enemy, but he was outnumbered. Marin and the other apprentices leaped into the fray, their own weapons held high. At the sight of them, Angus growled and set off after Zorzi, the youngest. He disarmed the boy, poised to join the battle.

Blaise was at his back in seconds. "Our deal is off, Angus! I should have known better…"

"What are you on about?" Angus muttered as he sliced at a wraith. He waded into the fray, swinging at Soranzo and his minions. "I swore an oath for you and I meant it!"

Blaise jumped back, chastened, and grabbed Sunni by the arm. He dragged her round the fight to Lorimer's side and they crouched down beside him.

With a mighty blow, Angus knocked Soranzo's blade from his hand. It skidded across the deck and landed at

Sunni's feet. Without hesitation, she picked it up and stood, holding the rapier out as a warning to anyone who dared come closer.

Soranzo glanced at her from under his hooded eyelids as his phantoms stopped fighting and formed a protective ring around him.

"Now is your chance to kill me, Bellini," he said smoothly. "Or you, Sunniva. I would enjoy watching you try and fail."

Blaise could see her knuckles were white and the weapon trembled in her hands.

"I'm not killing anyone," said Sunni.

"Death *will* come to you, Soranzo, without her assistance." Corvo gestured to Angus and the apprentices to surround them. "And your blood will not be on her hands."

"I disagree." Soranzo did not take his eyes off Sunni. "I think this girl wants to settle a score with me – if she dares."

"Sunni!" Angus, panting and sweating, was barely able to contain himself. "Just stand your ground."

Soranzo spread his arms out wide and gestured for the spectres to back off. "Come, any of you, run me through! I would rather perish in battle than face an unending sleep in this shadowland or become a misplaced skeleton in the twenty-first century."

Corvo's rapier dipped for a second, but he gathered himself and said, "Signore, there is another choice." He sheathed his rapier and pulled a small sheet of parchment from his doublet. As he began drawing with a stump of charcoal, a large black circular shape appeared on the deck. It had a small gap on one side. With each stroke Corvo drew, smaller concentric lines grew inside until the circle was filled up except for an empty centre point. *A labyrinth.*

Corvo nodded once and the labyrinth began to glow. "Walk it to the centre, Soranzo, and be returned to the place where you first used the Oculus to enter the shadowlands."

A crooked smile grew on Soranzo's face.

"You can't let him return to the past, sir," Blaise blurted out. "He'll decipher your clues and go after the paintings again!"

Corvo shook his head. "I did not say Soranzo would return to the year 1583 – just to his home."

The smile drained from his enemy's face.

"Walk to the centre of this labyrinth, signore. It will transport you to a year when you would have been a very old man. You will die instantly and peacefully on the other side."

"I will become a skeleton like the others," Soranzo muttered.

"But your family will bury you and tend your grave," Corvo answered. "Is that not better than your other choices?"

Soranzo considered this for a moment. Then, head rigidly high and eyes forward, he walked towards the labyrinth's entrance. The others all made way for him and the spectres followed at his shoulders. Without a word, he stalked round and round the labyrinth's path until he arrived at the centre and turned to face them. As he bent to take an exaggerated bow, his body evaporated into a wispy vapour and disappeared, taking the seven wraiths with him into the beyond. The labyrinth glowed a bit brighter for a moment and then faded to nothing.

There were sighs of astonishment and relief.

Angus dropped his weapon and held out his hands. "I guess I'm next, Signor Corvo. Send me back to my banishment on the island."

"No," said Corvo. "You are finished here. Everything is finished. I want you all out." He gestured for Sunni, Blaise and Lorimer to approach. Sunni carefully laid Soranzo's weapon on the floor and tiptoed over.

Blaise hadn't exactly expected thanks from Corvo but he also hadn't expected him to be so sullen either. "This is my fault, sir. My curiosity got the better of me."

"So did mine," said Lorimer sheepishly. "The wish to see your magical world overwhelmed my common sense. Stupidly, I thought there might be the slightest chance that I would find you, signore."

Blaise frowned. "But we told you we only met his doubles, Mr Bell."

"I know," the teacher answered, scratching the back of his neck nervously. "But I had to see for myself. I've dreamed for so long that I could somehow meet Signor Corvo and ask for my cousin Angus's freedom."

"You have it," Corvo said curtly.

Angus squeezed his eyes shut and nodded as Lorimer murmured, "Thank you."

"Signor Corvo," said Sunni. "We did keep your secrets, even when we nearly died for it. This wasn't the first time we met Soranzo. He came after us a few months ago."

Corvo put his hand up to stop her. "No stories. I believe you but I am tired. No more secrets. Find my three enchanted paintings and make sure they are safe. I hope they are still hidden somewhere in the real world, in your century. That is the last thing I ask."

"Under the Bright Ravens?" Blaise repeated.

"Yes. And you already have the cipher disc, I believe." Corvo managed a half-smile. "I will tell you no more than that because I cannot trust a Bellini." The magician raised his eyebrows and called his eldest apprentice. "Marin, you were very hard on these two children. Soranzo caused this trouble, not them. Their hearts are in the right place."

Lady Ishbel's spirit stood close behind Marin. "I am sorry," he said in a flat voice.

Sunni seemed unimpressed by this, and Blaise's heart leaped with satisfaction.

"Lady Ishbel is standing behind you, Marin," she said. "You know that, don't you?"

He nodded and looked at Corvo. "Her spirit will stay. I wish it."

"This means you'll leave me alone, Lady Ishbel," said Sunni. "Right?"

Ishbel's slender hand curled round Marin's arm and he covered it with his.

Corvo pointed at the ship tethered behind them. "Now go! Your way will be clear. Go before this shadowland turns dark again."

"What about you, sir?" Blaise asked meekly.

The sorcerer nodded at the sea stack. "We will return to our home in Arcadia."

Not daring to say anything else, Sunni, Blaise, Angus and Lorimer climbed onto the empty vessel. With a sweep of his arm, Corvo cut the invisible tethers and all the ships except his own spun away in a sudden whirlwind.

The rogue wind blew them back to the long quay. They quickly disembarked and hurried through the dark Amsterdam streets towards the house they had arrived in.

Blaise could barely recognise some streets without their foliage and hills, but there was no sign of any giant lurking tentacles under the bridge and, to his relief, the sea snake was gone. Just one full moon remained in the sky. He imagined the sea stack, and Corvo's lone ship still twinkling next to it, attracting everything alien to this shadowland in a spinning funnel and sending it back to where it belonged in Arcadia's living underworlds.

Chapter 24

"Don't let go of it!" Dean struggled to keep the wobbling table from collapsing as Munro grasped the hot Oculus with his gauntlet gloves.

"The roof's going to come down on us any minute," said the spirit photographer, straining to keep the magic lantern stable.

Someone had pounded on the door but there was no way Dean was letting anyone, even Mandy, interfere with this. He had yelled at them to go away, and that was that, though he suspected they'd be back if they dared come up through the crumbling building again.

The floor rocked and the walls shifted, sending the painted sea creatures on the oak ceiling beams into shudders.

"Hold on!" Dean shouted above the worrying creak of the rafters. "The projection is changing again."

"You said that ages ago," Munro bellowed.

"You know what the picture is supposed to look like, right?"

Munro hugged the Oculus as it bounced during another tremor. "I told you! It's a room with a bed and a candlestick on a table."

Dean coughed another helping of plaster dust out of his throat and said, "If I die and you don't, I'm going to haunt you like you won't believe!"

"Nice thought," shouted Munro. "No offence, but I'd rather keep you alive, which is why I think you should go while you can. I'll keep the Oculus steady."

Dean snorted. "No, I'm not leaving. This is a two-man job."

"I hope, wherever your stepsister is, she knows how lucky she is."

"When I see her, you can bet I'm going to remind her." He cowered as a chunk of plaster plummeted to the floor. "Wait, look at that!"

"Something's happening in the projection!" Munro cradled the magic lantern while trying to keep his face away from its heat.

The mish-mash of ciphers and symbols was giving way to something else.

"A picture!" Dean whooped as the image adjusted and clarified. He could hear a disturbance outside in the corridor and gritted his teeth. "People are coming again! What if they've got a key? What if they turn the light on?"

"I think things are settling down," Munro said, looking up at the painted creatures on the beams. They were still and showed no sign of ever having moved a millimetre. "The table's steady."

"No!" Dean said. "Don't let go yet."

The Amsterdam bedroom appeared in the projection but it was empty.

"Oh, man!" He bent his head down on the table, exhausted.

"This is good," said Munro cheerfully. "This is very good! Come on, look at the wall!"

Dean looked up and smiled at the image of Blaise rolling head first into the projection and pulling Sunni in behind him with a candlestick in her hand.

"Boy, she's in a right state!" Dean gasped, but he couldn't help grinning, especially when the two of them hauled Lorimer Bell into the picture. "That's it!" Without looking at the projection any longer, he yanked open the Oculus door and put the flame out with Munro's brass candlesnuffer.

The Mariner's Chamber went black and Munro staggered back onto the bench with an exclamation of relief. From somewhere in the dark a man groaned.

Dean switched on his torch and shone it at the place where the noises had come from. It picked up Lorimer Bell, curled up on his side with his eyes closed. Dean waved the torch across the rest of the floor, hunting for Sunni and Blaise. It took a moment to locate them because they were so quiet, but once he'd found them, he knew why. They were lost in a kiss, their arms tightly wrapped around each other.

Before he could make any embarrassing comments, Sunni reluctantly broke away and glared into the light. "Dean? What on earth are you doing here?"

"Saving you," said Dean.

She and Blaise got to their feet together. "Where's Munro?"

Dean swung the torch onto the spirit photographer's startled face.

"Why did you do it?" Blaise bore down on him. "I said not to aim the Oculus at the painting but you did it anyway! You dumped us right in it."

"Huh?" Dean grunted. "It's this guy's fault?"

"Pretty much!"

"I don't know what got into me," mumbled Munro.

"I think I do," said Sunni, coming up close to Blaise. "You thought you could get your hands on the three lost paintings."

Munro hung his head.

"Well, we didn't find them," said Blaise, putting his arm around Sunni's shoulders. "So too bad for you."

A key turned in the lock and overhead light flooded the Mariner's Chamber.

"Well, for the love of—" Jimmy the security guard said, clapping his hand to his forehead, before he was knocked out of the way by a small horde of people.

"Sunni!" Rhona bustled over, her expression a mix of relief and anger. She gave her stepdaughter a quick squeeze and gasped at her streaked face, torn gown and the filthy once-white cardigan. "What happened?"

"Here we go," Dean murmured. "Get ready, Sun."

"Rhona, Dad. We're okay." Sunni made no attempt to remove Blaise's arm as she reached out to her father. "Why are you here?"

Sunni's father put his arms around them both. "It got late so we came to give you a lift home. We found the Tower in chaos, rumbling and swaying like it was in an earthquake, and everybody running out. What on earth has been going on up here?"

"Dad, are you ready for another long story?" she asked sheepishly. "Like London?"

Her father sighed. "Not again."

"Afraid so. It's all to do with that." She pointed at the Oculus.

"Let's hear about it later. First, you owe Mandy your thanks." Sunni's father nodded at Mandy, who beamed. "If it hadn't been for her, we wouldn't have known where you were."

"Mandy!" Sunni gaped at her friend and the familiar cat in her arms.

"And I wouldn't have known if it hadn't been for Dean spying on you and Blaise," said Mandy. Everyone's heads swivelled towards Dean.

"You were the spy?" Blaise exclaimed. "You gave me the creeps, man. I couldn't stop looking over my shoulder!"

Dean shrugged, pleased at this compliment.

"He saved the day," Munro said mournfully. "You all have him to thank. If he and Mandy hadn't got in and found me…"

"I'll be having a word with you about that later, Munro," Jimmy interrupted, jangling his keys.

Mandy carried Lexie over to the spirit photographer, but he shook his head and said in a resigned voice, "I think she's chosen to stay with you now, if you'll have her." Mandy's purple zombie flesh reddened and she nodded.

Rhona crushed Dean in her arms. "I thought you were out at a Halloween party." Then she pulled back and frowned at his ninja gear. "You left the house as a pirate."

Dean shrugged again. "So I didn't stay a pirate."

His mother shook her head. "You lied to me, son."

"Yeah, I did. And I'm sorry. But it worked out, didn't it?" he pleaded.

"You lied as well, Sunni," her father said.

"About James!" Rhona exclaimed.

James looked up from the floor nearby where he, Iona and Aurora were tending to Lorimer and shook his head. "Yeah. Your stepmum thought I was taking you to the party."

Dean smirked. Sunni winced as though she had just got a cold blast from the freezer cabinet at the supermarket.

"Pardon?" she asked weakly.

"Thing is," said James. "It went viral. Iona's mum was onto my mum – you get the picture. Luckily Iona's cool about it."

Iona gave Sunni a frosty look.

"All right, it was a fib so I could come here tonight with Blaise. But I'm not going to lie about him any more!" Sunni put her arm around him and took a deep breath as she faced her dad and Rhona. "I want to be with Blaise. He's my best friend and I'm proud of it." She looked sideways at him and asked, "Is that okay with you?"

Blaise grinned. "Totally okay."

"I wouldn't want to be in danger with anybody else," she said.

"And I wouldn't have had the courage to keep going without Sunni being there," said Blaise, standing tall. "I'd never let anything bad happen to her either."

Rhona dragged Sunni to her and hugged her tight. "We just worry about you."

"I know," came Sunni's muffled voice. "What about Blaise?"

"We'll talk when we get home," said Rhona, giving him the beginning of a smile.

"Hey!" a gravelly voice interrupted. Looking half-conscious,

Angus stumbled to his feet and teetered slightly as he pointed a dirty finger at the bench.

Dean nearly croaked. How had that crook sneaked back in?

"Angus Bellini." Munro's mouth hung open.

"Why am I not surprised to see you here?" Angus said. "Little thief like you."

"No," Munro protested. "Not any more."

"Really." Angus fumed, moving towards the bench.

Sunni's father moved his family away from Munro and the others shuffled a few steps back.

Jimmy jumped in front of Angus with his arms up. "Stop right there."

"Angus." Lorimer dragged himself to standing. "Don't be stupid."

"I just want an answer from this dude," said Angus. "What are you doing here?"

"I came here to do some shows with my magic lantern," Munro murmured. "And take some photos."

Angus tore his hand through his unkempt hair. "And see what you could steal. Isn't that your thing, Munro? Shoplifting unusual gear?"

There was a collective draw of breath from everyone in the Mariner's Chamber.

"How do you know that?" Sunni asked.

"He and I have crossed paths before," said Angus.

"I'm on the straight and narrow now." Munro crossed his arms over his chest.

"Sure you are." Angus waved his arm at the Oculus. "Where did you get that?"

The spirit photographer set his lips in a thin line.

"You said you found it in Istanbul," Blaise said with distaste. "Bet that's not true either."

But Munro said nothing.

"The Oculus is stolen?" Sunni was outraged.

"Wouldn't surprise me at all," said Angus.

"Yeah?" said Dean. "And you're the good guy now?"

Angus gave him a sidelong glance. "Well, you've certainly grown since I last saw you, Deano." He held both his hands up. "No, I'm no good guy. In fact, you can call the police now, Mr Security Man. We're ready to go, right, Munro?"

The spirit photographer just shrugged.

"Angus Bellini. That's right, the one who put Mac into hospital last winter," Jimmy said into his phone. "And another one called Munro." He signed off and shouted above the buzz of voices, "I want the ladies and kids out now. If you gentlemen would be so kind as to stay behind and help me keep an eye on these two."

"Tell the cops to hurry, would you?" Angus groaned. "I'm desperate for a wash and some grub."

Rhona herded Sunni, Blaise, Dean and the other teenagers towards the door.

"Before you go," Munro said in a sepulchral tone from his place on the bench. "Can I just direct your attention to the walls and ceiling? Not a crack or fleck of plaster dust after this place nearly came down around us. But even stranger than that" – he lifted a gloved finger towards *The Mariner's Return to Arcadia* – "the painting's gone."

A collective roar rose up. The canvas was blank, as if there had never been a painting on it at all.

"I've spotted a lurker," said Blaise, nodding at the Wee Cuppa Café's picture window. "The hoodie staring in at us."

"I'll get him." Sunni hurried out of the café and called after the figure, which had turned to jog away. "Oh, come on, Dean, will you just get inside?"

Dean turned round to face her and shrugged.

"We want you to come in," she insisted. "I'll even buy you something to eat."

"All right." He strolled over with a grin.

She gave him a gentle shove through the door and over to their table. "I found the spy."

Blaise pulled a chair over for Dean. "I don't mind this guy." He pushed away his sketchbook, pencils and a circular brass object. It was made up of two discs, one larger on the bottom and a smaller one on top, with a red gemstone set in the centre. Both the outer and inner rings were etched with letters of the alphabet.

"What's that?" asked Dean, picking it up and rotating the inner wheel round.

"A cipher disc. People used these to break codes a long time ago," said Sunni. "Fausto Corvo's clones carried this one about in the projections we visited. We're going to have a go at deciphering some gobbledygook we saw in the shadowlands."

"Let's see it," said Dean. Blaise showed him the nonsense words from the hulls of the ships in Venice, on the basilisk sign in Prague and on the sketches in Amsterdam.

VYLNLUG LUVUHOM GUULN

VYLNLUG LUVUHOM UJLCF

VYLNLUG LUVUHOM GYC

"The first two words are the same in all three," said Dean.

Sunni rolled her eyes. "We'd got that far."

"Well, doesn't the cipher thing come with directions?"

"Yeah, we think it's based on the kind of cipher Julius Caesar used. The letters on the inside ring are the coded ones," she said. "So you line up the first letter of the code with the correct letter on the outside ring."

"How do you know what the correct letter is?" Dean asked.

"We don't," said Sunni. "We have to try each letter out one by one till we find the right combination."

Blaise got a clean sheet of a paper and a pencil. "So we start with A, the first letter of the alphabet." He lined up the V on the inner ring with A on the outer ring and wrote down 'A' on his paper. "Okay, so the next letter of the code is Y and that lines up with D on the outer ring." He wrote a D next to the A.

"I get it," said Dean. "That means the L in the code is Q on the outside ring. Then S and then Q again. Okay, I've got the answer. ADQSQZL."

Blaise crossed out the letters on his paper. "Well, that didn't work."

"So now line up the V with B, the next letter on the outer ring," said Dean.

"All right, boss," Blaise answered with a grin and rotated the inner ring one letter over. "V equals B. Then Y equals E. And L equals R." He carefully wrote each letter on the paper.

"BERTRAM," said Dean.

Blaise and Sunni looked at each other, astonished.

Blaise quickly figured out the last four letters on paper and said, "You're right, Dean. How did you do that so fast?"

"I play a lot of games."

"So the first word in the code is Bertram," said Blaise. "And I bet the second is Rabanus."

"Ravenous." Dean stretched and glared at Sunni. "I'm feeling pretty ravenous. Thought you were going to get me something to eat, Sun. I'll have a brownie."

"No, Rabanus, not ravenous," said Sunni slowly, with a puzzled look at Blaise.

"They sound they same," said Dean.

"Yeah, they do," she answered, grabbing her phone and punching something into it. After a few moments, she read, "*Rabanus*, from Old High German, meaning raven."

Dean whistled.

"What about Bertram?" asked Blaise, quickly working through the rest of the scrambled words on his sketchbook.

"Germanic," said Sunni excitedly. "Means bright raven."

"The name Corvo means raven too," said Dean.

"Yeah, and Corvo said to look for the three paintings under the Bright Ravens." Blaise held up his paper so they could see.

BERTRAM RABANUS MAART

BERTRAM RABANUS APRIL
BERTRAM RABANUS MEI

"Hold on," Sunni said, busy with her phone. "*Maart* is Dutch for March."

"And *April* is April?" smirked Dean.

"Brilliant, Dean." Sunni narrowed her eyes. "And *Mei* is May in Dutch too."

"Type in BERTRAM RABANUS MAART and see what it says," Blaise said.

After a few minutes Sunni's eyes grew wide and she held the phone up to show them a picture. "It's the title of this landscape painting by Bertram Rabanus."

"We saw a sketch of that in the Amsterdam projection!" said Blaise.

She scrolled to two more pictures. "These too. They're the sketches that had the codes on the back."

"Is there any information about Bertram?" Blaise asked.

"No. He's practically anonymous," said Sunni. "Just a signature on these paintings."

"I'll bet Bertram never existed." Blaise jabbed his finger into the paper. "He must have been Fausto Corvo. That workshop in Henryk's house must have been where Corvo worked while he was in Amsterdam."

"Covering up his three magical paintings with boring landscapes and signing them with the alias Bertram Rabanus," said Sunni.

She joined Blaise as he jumped up and swept his sketchbook and the cipher disc into his messenger bag. "Let's go," he said.

"Hey!" Dean exclaimed. "What are you doing?"

Sunni slapped some coins down on the table. "Get your brownie and come on!"

"Where?"

"My house," said Blaise, taking Sunni's hand with a smile. "We have to track down where those three landscapes are now."

"Because they have some pretty special under-paintings," Sunni said, tying her lavender-striped scarf around her neck.

The trio made their way into the early November evening and looked up. The sky was a canopy of celestial jewels sparkling on dark velvet, still, ancient and perfect.

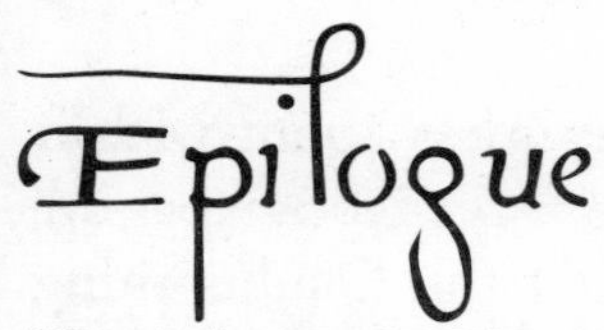

Epilogue

The Mariner's Chamber was peaceful at last. After weeks of investigations, the police had finally gone, shaking their heads at the blank canvas where Fausto Corvo's painting used to be. The castle's managers had fretted, distressed that their prize attraction had vanished and that Sir Innes Blackhope's will stated that nothing could be changed in that room. The blank canvas would have to stay as it was. So two cleaners swept the tiled floor and polished the picture frame, readying the chamber for reopening.

"This is ridiculous," one said as they replaced the rope barrier in front of the empty canvas. "Who's going to come here to see a blank picture?"

"The same people who come to look at that," replied the other, nodding at the floor where the tiled labyrinth had been before it faded away.

"It's daft," scowled the first cleaner. "Looking at nothing!"

"People like the mystery of this place." The second cleaner shrugged. "It's the Blackhope enigma."

"I guess you're right. We've got visitors already," said the first cleaner as Sunni, Blaise and Dean ventured through the door. "Yes, you can come in. We're just leaving."

When the cleaners had gone, the trio walked up to the blank canvas on the wall.

"It's really weird seeing it blank," said Blaise, touching his hand to his chest. "It kind of hits me here."

"Me too," said Dean. "We were inside that painting once and now it's disappeared."

"Corvo made sure no one can ever mess about with it again," said Sunni.

"Good," said Dean. "And good that the Oculus thing went to the Corvo museum so no one else can get their dodgy hands on it!"

"Yeah, but what about the lost paintings?" Blaise turned to Sunni. "We're doing the right thing, aren't we? Not telling anyone that we've located them?"

Dean jumped in. "That's Corvo's secret. No one can know but us!"

"He's right," said Sunni. "We promised we'd find them and make sure they were safe. And they are. And that's all Corvo wanted." The magician would have been pleased to see the Dutch museum where his three disguised masterpieces had ended up, with its state-of-the-art security and keen guards.

Blaise nodded. "Just making sure neither of you changed your mind."

"No way," she answered. "We can't let him down now. What if we tell, and criminals steal them? They're safe where they are, hidden under the Rabanus paintings."

"I sure hope so." Blaise gave the blank canvas a long look then turned away. "Well, we're done here, I guess. There's nothing left to see."

"Yeah." Sunni said, biting her lip as she followed him out. "The magic's all gone."

But Dean lingered by the canvas, staring at it. "Uh, you'd better get back here."

Together they peered at the surface.

"What?" asked Blaise.

"Keep watching," Dean whispered. "There!"

Something small and pale grey appeared on the blank canvas, moving slowly and smoothly, like an object just visible in the fog. Its outline became clearer as it travelled with long strokes of its feathered wings.

"A raven," Sunni breathed. "Corvo's world is still there, somewhere deep down."

The raven glanced out at them for a moment. Then, within the blink of an eye, it wheeled and soared away into the canvas's infinite whiteness.

THE END

Q & A with

Teresa Flavin

What gave you get the idea for this book?

After *The Crimson Shard*, there were still mysteries about Fausto Corvo, Soranzo and the three magical paintings for Sunni and Blaise to solve. As I am very interested in magic lanterns and other devices that entertained people before movies were invented, like the *camera obscura*, *zoetrope*, *phenakistoscope*, *thaumatrope* and *zoopraxiscope* (you can find great examples of these on the Internet), I was really keen to feature a magic lantern in this story. I also wanted to bring the adventure back to Blackhope Tower, but this time, set it at Halloween so I could include some ghostly characters. As soon as I imagined Munro appearing at Blackhope Tower with Corvo's Oculus, the story began to take shape.

Was there an Oculus in real life?

Sadly not! The Oculus is from my imagination, but it is based on actual inventions that projected images. For many centuries, would-be magicians had been creating the illusions of spirits and demons using mirrors, glass lenses and clever lighting. In Holland in the sixteenth century, the production of lenses improved, which then led to the development of the telescope and microscope in the early seventeenth-century. Better glass lenses also brought about more convincing special effects for showmen to use.

It is believed that the first person to create a portable magic lantern was a Dutch scholar named Christiaan Huygens, in the mid-1600s. As information about his device spread, others, such as the famous German scholar Athanasius Kircher, began developing their own magic lanterns and painted glass slides to create shows that would astonish audiences. Over the following centuries, magic lantern technology grew more and more sophisticated. By the 1890s, magic lanterns were at the height of their popularity, but soon began to die out with the invention of films.

Today magic lanterns and their slides are collectors' items. If you do a search for magic lanterns on the Internet, you will find fantastic examples from over the centuries – and you might even find a vintage magic lantern performance in a museum or gallery near you.

Were magic lantern slides really as scary as the ones Munro showed?

Absolutely! Painted slides were much like the ones Munro showed in the Oculus, with pictures of skeletons, witches and monsters. As the technology improved, showmen presented ever more dramatic magic lantern performances designed to spook people. One seventeenth-century travelling showman had a 'lantern of fear', which he claimed featured the appearance of Death itself.

Have you ever seen a ghost or spirit?

I have never been lucky enough to see one, but I believe that I may have heard one or two on my travels. While I was staying in an old English inn, I was awoken late in the night by footsteps pacing back and forth in the room above me, only to learn later that there was nothing up there but an empty attic space! And, another time, I stayed in a Scottish castle where the temperature dropped suddenly in one corridor – right next to a particularly creepy old portrait.

Was Emperor Rudolf II a real person?

Yes, he lived from 1552-1612 and was ruler of one of the most powerful European empires of the time. Under his reign, Prague became known as the 'Golden City', attracting great artists and scholars as well as magicians.

Rudolf was fascinated with art, alchemy, astronomy and all the new knowledge that the Renaissance had cultivated. He obsessively collected magical and scientific curiosities from around the world and built royal workshops in Prague castle, where artists and craftsmen produced large quantities of artworks for him. He even had agents that travelled around Europe seeking new paintings and sculptures for his collections.

Fausto Corvo would have been very keen to give his three paintings to a patron like Emperor Rudolf, who would have appreciated their artistic and magical brilliance.

What is a cipher disc?

It is a tool for creating and deciphering codes. The cipher disc was designed in the mid-fifteenth century by Leon Battista Alberti, a talented Italian architect and philosopher. It is made up of two discs, one larger than the other. Each disc has letters of the alphabet marked around its edge, with upper case letters on the larger disc and lower case letters on the smaller one. When the smaller disc is rotated and a lower case letter is lined up with an upper case letter on the larger ring, codes can either be created or deciphered.

In *The Shadow Lantern*, the code Fausto Corvo used was relatively simple, but the Alberti cipher disc could also be used to make much more complex codes.

Acknowledgements

I would like to thank the entire Templar Publishing team for their enthusiasm and support for *The Shadow Lantern* and for the previous two books in this trilogy, *The Blackhope Enigma* and *The Crimson Shard*. My editors, Anne Finnis and Emma Goldhawk, gave me invaluable guidance throughout the revision process. Fiction designer Will Steele helped make my illustrations look as fine as possible. I am particularly grateful to The Parish's Tom Sanderson for designing all three book jackets so beautifully. I am thrilled every time I look at them.

The team at Candlewick Press have done a wonderful job adapting my books for North American readers. Many thanks to my editor, Kate Fletcher, for all her work.

My agent, Kathryn Ross, has been my stalwart supporter and adviser throughout the creation of the trilogy. I'm grateful for her good humour, wise perspective and all the hard work she does on my behalf.

When I embarked on telling the story of Sunni and Blaise's adventures, I was not sure I would publish one novel, let alone three. Fortunately, I share the path with my husband, Pablo, whose love and encouragement keep me going. I deeply appreciate his support and that of family and friends worldwide.

A huge thank you goes out to my readers, young and old. I have been touched by your messages, cards and letters from around the globe. It gives me so much pleasure to know that you enjoy my stories and I'm looking forward to bringing you new ones in the future.